CHRISTMAS EVE
on the
Underground Railroad
and Other Christmas Stories

Michael Easterling

VALLEY OAK PUBLICATIONS

For my parents, Albert Crayton Easterling
and Marjorie Jane Easterling

Table of Contents

Christmas Eve on the Underground Railroad

melia, my great, great, granddaughter, insists upon reading me the newspaper each day. She says it is important that I stay conversant with world affairs. I would remind Amelia that there is "nothing new under the sun," save that I would appear unappreciative to this kindhearted young woman who embodies all that is good in us as Friends.

This morning's news is of the dedication of the memorial to Abraham Lincoln erected in our nation's capital. As I stare at the sea of faces in the newspaper photograph, I wonder how many are old enough to remember slavery. I wish I had not the memory of it. To witness a wretched fugitive being half dragged behind the horse of a slavecatcher is an experience that burrows into the mind and remains there forever.

Emily asks for my thoughts as I continue to stare at the photograph, and I share with her my curiosity as to whether anyone in the crowd remembers the dark days well before the Civil War when the power of the slave owners seemed insurmountable. None could remember unless nearly as old as I am, and I am one hundred and two, though there was a time, working on the underground railroad, when I thought I would not live past the age of seven and twenty!

Knock! Knock! Knock!

"Who goes there?"

"A friend with friends."

Those who served on the underground railroad used code words or phrases to distinguish friend from enemy. Fugitive slaves were called "passengers"; those who helped them along the road to freedom were "conductors"; a "friend with friends" meant a conductor with passengers needing a "station", a place to hide.

One evening, in the year 1847, a woman previously known to me, Laura Haviland her name, arrived at my door and spoke those words, "a friend with friends." It was Christmas Eve, and I was preparing to spend the evening in the company of Friends.

I opened the door and stepped out onto the porch. "Laura, what can this be? I was just leaving to–"

She seized me by the arm before I could finish. "Quick, John, there's not a moment to lose! The slavecatchers are close on our heels!" As she spoke, she fairly dragged me in the direction of the horse barn.

I opened the barn door and held a lighted match to the lantern hanging within. Huddled on the floor were a negro man and woman. The man, whose skin was the darkest I had ever seen, rose as I approached. He was dressed in scant little considering the time of year: no shoes, thin homespun trousers tied with a drawstring, a shirt, much too large, torn in places and revealing the great muscles of his arms and shoulders. Though exhaustion showed in his face, his eyes were lit with defiance.

The woman was more warmly clothed. She had a scarf tied around her head, a loose apron over her coarse woolen dress, and old boots upon her feet, perhaps the cast-offs of a small man or a boy. Around her shoulders was draped a shawl covered with bits of twigs and leaves. She was stout and more light-skinned than the man.

Of course, all this I recalled afterwards. Then my only concern was that the woman was moaning low and continuously and, now and then, crying out loudly as if in pain.

I turned to the man. "What ails her?"

Behind me Laura spoke. "She is with child, John."

I whirled about to face Laura. "What? Has thee lost thy reason? Bringing a woman like this here? She is a great danger to us all!" As proof of this, the woman suddenly cried out louder than before!

Then the man spoke. His voice was low and his words came slowly as he struggled with the few words of English he knew. "My son... he... no born... slave!" He stood there with both hands in front of his face, as if in supplication, yet each hand was a clenched fist, and in the glow of the lantern light, I could not but notice the wide scars around each wrist.

Laura spoke anxiously, "We must help them, John, and quickly!"

I know I heeded her words, yet I remember feeling frozen with fear. I found the small door behind the corn crib, the one I thought myself so clever in the making since no one could see its opening. For certain, I had sheltered passengers before–for a night, perhaps

two, when it was safe to do so. In my mind, I knew slavery was wrong, for in the Bible it is written that all men are of the same blood. Upon occasion, a slavecatcher might stop at my house, seeking information, believing that, as a Friend, I was compelled to speak the truth. Yet I was certain that no slavecatcher suspected me of harboring a fugitive, and certainly never like this, a woman great with child and the slavecatchers in close pursuit! Furthermore, the hiding place was made to hide bodies, but could not conceal the voice of a woman crying out in pain!

As the man began to help his wife through the opening, I stopped them both. I placed my hands upon the woman's shoulders and shook her until her pain-glazed eyes focused upon mine.

"Thee must shut thy mouth!" I said as loudly as I dared, and I shook her harder, "Woman, shut thy mouth!" I pushed an angry finger into the man's chest. "Thee must make her shut her mouth!" It was a sin to have acted thus in anger, but such was the power of the fear within me.

I closed the door upon them and quickly spread hay upon the floor to cover footprints. It was then that we heard the sound of horses coming into the yard. I took the lantern, and both Laura and I went out to meet the slavecatchers. There was no pity in the faces of the six men who sat upon exhausted horses, one whose mouth bled from the bit having cut. Neither was there any "by your leave," for having come uninvited and unannounced. Such men as these men were deemed outcasts even among those who saw not the evil of

slavery. Often they were paid for their services through intermediaries to spare the slave owner the unpleasantness of associating with them, and by this arrangement was the slave owner also spared the sight of what befell the unfortunate fugitives between the time of their capture and their return.

A ruffian, a little better dressed than the others, served as their leader. "We're lookin' for two runaway niggas, a boy and his woman. We judge you're hidin' 'em here."

Neither Laura nor I spoke.

The leader spat on the ground. "We plan to tear this here place inside out 'less'n you tell us where you're keeping them."

I thought not to reason with him. In truth, I was frightened beyond reason. It must be understood the penalties for harboring a fugitive slave. At that time, the slave owners' power was such that they determined the law, and the law stated that a man caught helping a slave escape could be sent to prison and all he owned confiscated. But slavecatchers often acted outside the law and were wont to mete out far worse punishments, even to the point of killing those who helped the negro.

I told myself it was hopeless, certain any moment the negro woman, in her distress, would cry out, and the slavecatchers find the hiding place. I told myself that if I gave up the fugitives before the slavecatchers found them on their own, they might take them and leave Laura and me unharmed. Reasoning thus, I knew that I would give up the man and woman. And in that instant, even as I opened

my mouth to utter the words of betrayal... I was made anew.

From whence came the other voice? I know that voice which ceaselessly babbles within my mind all my waking hours, and this voice sounded like that, yet different, not just a voice, but a touch which enfolded me and held me and pressed upon every particle of my skin as it spoke but two words: *Fear not*, and being held in the love of His embrace, I did not fear.

Then the iron entered my soul!

"Who are you?" I cried out! I quickly handed the lantern to Laura then strode among them and many of the riders wheeled their horses about, much taken aback by my boldness. I fixed my eyes upon each man in turn, and whereas before I had only seen hard and cruel men, I now saw them for what they were: lost souls, crippled by hatred. I had thought them savage hunters, yet realized it was they who must hide from God.

"Who are you to bring us this trouble?" I shouted. "Would men of God profane this sacred night with such evil doing?" I turned to their leader. "Thee tells me why thee has come. I answer thee that if I had one hundred fugitives hidden, I would not give up a hair from one, even if thee should tear down my house and take my life, for the word of God sings in my heart that all men are equal in his eyes!"

I turned away and went to stand beside Laura. In a quieter, yet still spirit-filled voice, I said, "God stands beside us! Go you and return to your homes. Take your anger and leave us, for surely what you do is wicked in God's eyes!"

They understood me. They sensed a great spirit upon me. But they did not go.

Their leader dismounted and came forward. In his hand, he held a stout cudgel rudely carved from a tree knot. I extended my right arm to ward off his attack, and, quick as a cat, he brought the cudgel down upon my hand. The force of the stroke, and the pain of it, drove me to my knees.

Laura was at once beside me, shining the lantern down upon me. "Look thee! Thee has spoiled his hand, forever having use of it!"

"I want them niggas!" spat out the man.

Slowly, I rose to my feet, and with my hand not injured, I snatched the cudgel from the man's hand and threw it into the night. My action had caught him unawares. We stood unmoving, staring into each other's eyes, his filled with hatred, mine with righteous power. There was a stillness in the air. Being winter, no insect was awake to make a sound. Not a murmur came from the barn. All was quiet, even the horses, and in that silence, Laura moved between the man and myself.

"I tell thee the truth," she said, "there are no slaves here."

The man slowly turned to look upon Laura, then, just as slowly, turned back to me. Meeting his angry stare, I nodded my head in agreement. It was a ruse used before by other Friends. We believe in telling the truth in all things, but we also believe that no man is a slave to another. Thus, to say there were no slaves here was to speak truth.

The man ground the heel of one boot into the hard earth,

deciding. Then he whirled about, mounted his horse, and the slavecatchers rode out of the yard. We waited, listening to the sound of horse hooves fading in the distance.

Laura gently laid her hand upon my shoulder. "How is thy hand, John?"

The blood had begun to congeal, and I could move my fingers a little. "The pain of it was not as bad as I feared when I first beheld his cudgel."

Laura sighed. "John, what came over thee?"

A welcome gust of cold air blew across my face. I closed my eyes. My energies were spent, the elation gone, but not the knowing, and not the love. I looked to the heavens where a wandering star shone brightly in the twilight. "I received a great opening of God's word, and it has entered into my heart."

Silence then. The silence of understanding.

We waited a little longer, fearing the slavecatchers might return. In that time, I eased the skin back over my damaged hand and tied it with a handkerchief. Then we went to the barn. Laura entered before me, and I closed the door behind us as she took the lantern to the hiding place. I heard the sound of the door being opened, then Laura's gasp.

I hurried to the dark hiding place and looked within. The man was kneeling beside the woman who sat, leaning against him. Cradled in her arms was a baby. With eyes closed, the newborn child lay softly breathing, a tiny hand opening and closing upon the folds of his

mother's dress. The mother's face, covered with sweat, and the father's, the fear gone, revealed their joy as, by the light of the lantern, they looked upon their son for the first time.

Laura and I looked at each other and were of the same thought: how could this be? A mother giving birth, and a baby newborn, and yet we had not heard a sound? And now only this sweet vision of peace: father, mother, and child.

Over the next fifteen years, I lost count of the number of passengers I helped along the road from bondage to freedom, welcoming all who sought refuge, regardless of their condition or their number.

No longer had I fear of slavecatchers, for I had this to sustain me: that once upon a cold winter's night two miracles occurred; the first, that a man, who knew naught but by his small reason, was touched in his heart by an eternal love; the second, that in a world torn asunder by hatred and anger, God held apart a small, quiet place and gave to it his loving protection, and in that place, a child was born who would become a great leader to his people.

The Phillibrat

"I suppose you'll have to invite the Phillip brat," Steve said, only the way he ran the words together it came out "Phillibrat."

Mary, standing before the kitchen sink, looked out the window to her next-door neighbors' house wherein resided the Phillibrat. "I can hardly invite Laporsha and Titia to the children's Christmas party, and not invite Phillip."

Steve brought dirty dishes from the table. "Then maybe I should call Mr. Rossi and have our homeowner's insurance increased."

"Very funny," Mary replied.

"I'm not kidding. I wouldn't put it past the kid to break every stick of furniture we have."

"Sissy will keep an eye on Phillip, and there'll be other parents as well."

Steve took a washrag and started to run it over the stove top. "The Robinsons are saints. I would have given up on Phillip after the first week."

Mary sighed. It was hard to believe a ten-year-old boy could be so unremittingly angry and destructive.

"What are you thinking?" Steve said.

"Oh, just about Phillip. Do you remember that picture of the

governor holding Phillip's hand?"

"How could I forget? It was probably in every newspaper in the country. A teary-eyed governor holding the hand of a stone-faced kid. If you ask me, Phillip was already a hard case before the bombing took his parents."

Mary began to place dishes into the dishwasher. "I don't think so. You remember the funeral? The governor, the legislature, Senator Bolling, Congressman Mattingly, probably over 3,000 mourners, not to mention all the press?"

"What's your point?"

"Well, during all that public outpouring of grief was there ever a private moment when a lonely boy could cry over the death of his parents? Has there ever been a time?"

"All the victims' survivors got counseling," Steve said.

"It's not the same."

"Maybe. But one thing I know is the kid's dangerous. Or have you forgotten the cat?"

"Please, don't remind me!" Yet, there it was, the awful memory, the Robinsons hosting a Fourth-of-July barbeque. All had been going well until Phillip picked up the Robinsons' cat, who had been rubbing against his legs, and casually tossed him on the flaming grill.

Mercifully, the memory was disrupted by the sound of her children, Ellen and Roger, pounding across the upstairs floor. Drying her hands as she walked, Mary went into the living room and called up the stairs. "Hey you two! We let you out of dishes so you could

study. If you're done, I can find some other chores for you to do."

Instant silence.

Mary returned to the kitchen. "Steve, let's not worry about Phillip. It's going to be a great Christmas party. Just worry about your part. Have you talked to Walter about getting off work early?"

"Yeah, no problem. I told Walt I needed the extra time to harness my reindeer to the sleigh." Steve looked down at his stomach which pooched out over his belt. "Pretty soon, I won't need any padding to fit into the Santa suit."

"Remember," Mary said, "you're to make your entrance right after the storyteller is done, so you need to be here and in costume no later than say… three o'clock." She looked up at the clock. "Speaking of time, I still haven't finished the invitations, and I've got papers to grade!"

Every year, Mary gave a Christmas party for her children and their friends, usually on the first Monday of Christmas vacation. There were games, a gift exchange, and, of course, lots of delicious food and drink. And each year she tried to do something special. Last year it had been a taffy pull–messy, but fun. This year, she had hired a professional storyteller. She was taking a chance, never having met the fellow, but after reading several favorable on-line reviews, she gave him a call. His voice, spoken with a western twang, sounded friendly and relaxed. He was very clear about the services he provided. Still, after she hung up the phone, she had said a silent prayer. *Please God, don't let him say anything too adult for the children. Just a*

nice, simple, sweet Christmas story.

The next morning, before leaving for work, Mary was about to place the party invitations in her mailbox for the mail carrier to collect when she spied Phillip standing at the edge of the Robinsons' front porch, watching her. Suddenly, she felt apprehensive about leaving the invitations in the mailbox where Phillip could get them.

She had an idea. She walked towards the Robinsons' house, sorting through the invitations as she went. When she got to their porch, she stopped and handed one up to Phillip, who was standing at the top of the steps.

"Here, I should have thought of this before and saved myself a stamp."

Phillip, tall for his age, slender, strong, with fine, black, curly hair and skin like polished ebony, did not reach out to take the letter. "What is it?"

"It's an invitation to a Christmas party we're having a week from Monday."

"Am I invited?"

"Of course. It'll be lots of fun, and everyone you know will be there." Mary was still holding the invitation out to Phillip. "Phillip, will you take this before my arm falls off?"

Phillip pinched the corner of the letter between his thumb and index finger. "Woman, do you think I give a damn about some Santa Claus party?" He flicked his wrist and sent the letter whizzing over Mary's head in the direction of the trash bins. Then he turned and

walked back into the house, slamming the door behind him.

Mary fought to control her anger. She desperately wanted to rush after Phillip, grab him by his curly locks, drag him outside, and make him pick up the invitation. Then she smiled, thinking of how Phillip must have thought he was talking "macho male."

Well, 'woman', she told herself, *you best get your butt in gear or you'll be late for work.*

On the day of the Christmas party, the house looked wonderfully festive. A bushy Scotch pine stood in the corner of the living room, dripping with miniature lights, brilliant glass ornaments, and yards of popcorn strung together. The dining room table was loaded with plates of cookies, cakes, candies, and a large ceramic punch bowl for the hot apple cider. About an hour before the party was to begin, there was a knock on the kitchen door. Mary opened it to find Sissy Robinson standing there with a large tray of cookies.

"Merry Christmas!" Sissy said, a large smile on her tired face.

As Sissy passed through the door, Mary relieved her of the tray. "Are these your famous almond snowflake cookies?"

"Of course," replied Sissy with a laugh.

"Thank you so much." Mary set the tray on the kitchen counter and gave her friend a big hug then continued to hold Sissy close, sensing her need for comforting. Mary knew Sissy to be the most compassionate, fun-loving spirit ever packaged within a character made of steel. But today she seemed particularly troubled.

"Sit down and I'll pour us some coffee," Mary said.

Sissy sat down on one of the stools at the kitchen counter while Mary poured coffee into two fancy china cups. She also peeled back the plastic wrap on the tray of almond snowflake cookies and placed several on a plate. "I don't suppose anyone will notice a few of these cookies have gone missing."

"Lawd, chile, I made twelve dozen! If those kids eat all those cookies along with that pile of goodies you always have for them, we'll have to give them all insulin injections before we can send them home." Sissy took a sip of hot coffee then sighed.

Mary looked at her friend. "It's Phillip, isn't it?"

Sissy nodded. "His teacher called me today. She's going to recommend Phillip be placed in a special ed. class for the severely emotionally disturbed–at least for a part of the day." Sissy took another sip of coffee, then set her cup back down. "Of course, I can't blame her. Phillip has been disruptive all year. I'm sure there's not one of her students that he hasn't picked a fight with. It's just…what's the point? I know that child, and putting him in a special ed. class isn't going to change his behavior." Sissy ran both hands through her short, graying hair. "I'm losing him, Mary. I thought that with enough love and affection he would heal. But it's just not working. Every day, he retreats deeper inside himself. And it's getting harder and harder to cope with his anger. My sainted husband hasn't said a word against Phillip, but we both recognize how the stress of caring for Phillip has affected our girls. I'm afraid that, barring some

miracle, we're going to have to ask the county to find some other placement for him."

Mary placed her hand upon Sissy's. "I'm sure they couldn't find a family that could give him more loving attention than your family has."

"You've got that right." Sissy looked through the doorway at the Christmas tree, not really seeing it. "If I could just find the key to Phillip–something which would open up the goodness I know he's got in him, and let out all that anger." Sissy pushed up off the stool. "Grammy's watching Phillip; I'd best go rescue her. The girls are so excited about the party. Just wait until you see the dresses they made. They look like little angels."

By two-thirty, all the guests had arrived except the Robinsons. From past experience, Mary knew how to organize the party and delegate responsibility. Under the supervision of a couple of parents, the children had started to play a game in the living room. This left Mary available to keep things running smoothly and to take care of little emergencies should they occur. As she stirred the apple cider heating on the stove, there was a knock on the kitchen door followed by Sissy herding her children inside.

Mary stopped stirring to welcome her guests. "My goodness, you girls look absolutely stunning!" Laporsha wore a dress of red velvet trimmed with white lace. Titia's dress was all of white satin with a blue sash. "And to think you made those dresses yourselves!"

"With a little help from their grammy," Sissy said. She handed

Mary three wrapped presents, which Mary placed on one end of the counter alongside the others for the gift exchange.

"Phillip, you look very handsome," Mary said. He was wearing a pair of gray slacks and a white, long-sleeve shirt underneath a red V-neck sweater-vest. He ignored the compliment.

The sound of music issued from the living room.

"It sounds like you three are just in time for a game of musical chairs. Why don't each of you take a folding chair from the stack there and go join the fun?"

The two girls each rushed to join the game while Phillip opened a chair and sat down at the dining room table. He picked up a cookie and began to eat it. Then he picked up a spoon and began softly tapping it against the side of the empty cider bowl. It made a nice bell-like tone.

Ignoring the tapping, Mary went back to stirring the cider on the stove. The tapping got louder.

"Phillip, don't hit that bowl too hard," Mary said. "You might break it."

Ignoring her, Phillip continued tapping on the bowl.

"Boy, didn't you hear what Mrs. McNeil said?" Sissy said. "Now, take your chair and go into the room with the others!"

Ever so slowly, Phillip obeyed.

Sissy turned to Mary. "That's my boy." Changing the subject, she said, "Do you need any help?"

"No, I've got things pretty much under control. I'm just stirring

this cider while I'm waiting for the storyteller to arrive."

From the living room came the clash of chair being knocked over. "Phillip, that was my chair!" an angry child yelled. Sissy sighed, then went to deal with Phillip.

In a little while, the music began again. As Mary stirred the cider, half listening to the chorus of *Jingle Bells*, the light in the kitchen suddenly went dim. Looking up, Mary saw a man whose frame completely filled the window in the kitchen door. She quickly set down her stirring spoon and went to open the door.

"Mrs. McNeil?" the man said.

"Yes?"

"I'm Wendell Jones, the storyteller you talked to on the phone."

Mary stared at him. From his leather boots to his wide-brimmed hat, the top of which was hidden by the door frame, he was dressed like a cowboy in worn blue jeans, a red gingham shirt beneath a sheep-skin vest, and a large red bandana fastened around his neck with a silver clasp. The weathered condition of his face gave the impression of his being a rough character, but this was belied by a deep reservoir of humor in his pale blue eyes. In his left hand, Wendell held a beat-up guitar. But the most unusual aspect of his appearance was the saddle balanced upon his right shoulder.

Mary was unaware she had been staring.

Used to the effect his appearance had on people, Wendell Jones emitted a warm, infectious laugh. "May I come in?"

"Oh, sorry, of course." Mary opened wide the door.

Wendell ducked under the door frame then leaned his guitar against a wall before lowering his saddle to the floor. He extended a beefy hand towards Mary. "Wendell Jones, cowboy raconteur and poet, at your service."

Mary shook hands, hers being entirely engulfed by Wendell's. "Mary, um…Mary McNeil." She couldn't help but notice the colorful tattoo that spilled from underneath Wendell's shirt cuff. *Oh, brother, the kids are going to love this character.*

"Mary's a fine name," Wendell said. "Just call me Wendy—all my friends do. Sometimes, they also call me 'Windy' especially when my stories go on a bit." He laughed again and Mary couldn't help but laugh with him.

Getting into the spirit of the act, Mary pointed to the saddle. "So did you leave your horse hitched to the rail outside, partner?"

"I'm afraid it's just a prop, Mary. I ain't been in the saddle since I popped my knees herding mustangs out in Nevada many a year ago. Fact is, it's because of my knees that I bring the saddle along. When I'm tellin' stories to children, I'm usually down on the floor or ground. I find if I can sit on my saddle, instead of the floor, my knees don't complain so much."

There was a sudden burst of children's laughter from the other room.

"Sounds like you got a sizeable herd in there," Wendy said.

"They're playing games. When they're done, I thought it would be a good time for you to begin."

Remembering the cider, Mary quickly went back to the stove and starting stirring it again.

"Whatever it is you're cooking smells mighty good," Wendy said.

"Forgive me, I've had so much on my mind, I've forgotten my manners. Please sit down, Wendy, and let me pour you a cup of this cider." As she brought the cup to him she added, "I'll get you some cookies to go with this."

"Just this here cider will do me fine, Mary. I might have some of those cookies after my little performance, but I don't want to be choking on any crumbs when I'm talking. But this cider, now...it feels real good on the throat."

Laporsha came into the kitchen and was startled to see Wendell seated at the counter.

"Hey there, young 'un." Wendy said.

"Laporsha, this is Mr. Wendell Jones. He's going to be telling us stories soon."

"Hi," Laporsha said, in a quiet voice.

"What's up, honey?" Mary said.

"Mrs. Markham said to tell you that we're almost done playing games."

"Reckon it's show time," Wendy said, setting his cup down and reaching for his hat.

"Just set a spell, Wendell," Mary said. "I want the children to get a plate of goodies and a cup of cider before you start." *Set a spell?*

Now, I'm starting to sound like a cowboy.

Phillip managed to be first in line when Mary brought the bowl of hot cider to the dining room table. "Careful not to spill," she said, as she ladled cider into his cup.

Phillip shot her a look of pure hatred.

Oh, well, the carpet takes stains pretty well.

Having finished pouring cider for everyone, she returned to the kitchen. "They're ready for you, Wendy. Shall I give you an introduction?"

Wendy stood and picked up his guitar and saddle. "Just tell 'em my name and that I'm here to tell some stories."

Mary entered the living room. "Okay everyone. Let me have your attention." The children grew quiet. "I think you're in for a real treat, a gentleman who is going to tell us some stories. Please welcome, Mr. Wendell Jones."

She had barely gotten "Jones" out of her mouth when Wendy let loose with an ear-splitting "Yee haw!"

Mary jumped a foot, much to the delight of the children.

Wendy dropped his saddle on the floor then slowly settled down on top of it. "Howdy there, young'uns! I always like to start off these shindigs with a song. This is a real good one that was first sung by a cowpoke, name of Gene Autry. Now, you all know it, so I want you to help me by singing along. It's called Rudolph the Red-Nosed Reindeer."

Wendy had a surprisingly mellow voice, very pleasant to listen

to, and the children eagerly sang with him. When they came to the part about Rudolph making history, Wendy started to yodel. The children became so excited, Sissy had to shush them.

Mary was enjoying the performance as much as the children, yet something in the back of her mind was nagging at her. *Isn't there something I'm supposed to be doing?* Then it hit her! *Steve! Where is he?* It was then that the phone decided to ring. She ran to the kitchen and caught it before the third ring.

"Steve?"

"How did you guess?"

"Where are you?"

"Some garage in Denton. I was on the way home when all this steam started coming from under the hood. I think it's the water pump. A mechanic is looking at it now."

Oh, well. So much for Santa.

"I'm sorry, hon, I know you were counting on me."

"It's not the end of the world. The children are enjoying this storyteller so much, they probably won't notice Santa's absence. How are you getting home?"

"Walt's still at the office. I'll give him a call, and he can pick me up on his way home."

"All right. I'm glad it was nothing worse than a water pump."

"Me, too. I'll see you about six, okay?"

"Okay."

Mary returned to the doorway into the living room where she

could hear Wendy.

"Now, let me tell you about winters up there in west Montana," Wendy said. "Folks there used to joke that Santa wouldn't come Christmas Eve 'cause it's too cold for him, and Santa lives at the North Pole! So, that gives you an idea just how cold it gets.

"So Ike was headed back to his homestead, his team of horses pulling his sled across the hard, icy snow. He could tell by the way the sled creaked and groaned every time it went over a bump that it wouldn't be long before that old sled would only be fit for firewood."

Mary listened with half an ear, still thinking about the unused Santa suit lying on her bed. She looked out the living room window and saw a man bent over the hedge he was trimming. It was Mr. Woodworth, the gardener. She had a sudden idea and hurried back into the kitchen and out the door.

"Excuse me," she called, "Mr. Woodworth?"

The man stood up and turned toward her. It wasn't Mr. Woodworth.

Mary halted. "Oh, I'm sorry. I thought you were our gardener, Mr. Woodworth."

The man smiled. "Woody was feeling a little under the weather and asked if I'd pinch hit for him. My name's Sanford. What can I do for you?"

Sanford, Mary noticed, was much older than Mr. Woodworth, and not very neat in appearance. With his unkempt beard and his straggly white hair spilling from under a woven cap, he looked a wild

man. Yet put him in a Santa suit…

Oh, why not? If I can let a giant cowboy loose in my house, why not a wild man gardener?

Mary quickly explained the situation.

"So, you want me to play Santa and pass out some presents?"

"The children would love it if you would."

Sanford laughed then lowered his hedge trimmers to the ground. "Well, why not? Playing Santa sounds a lot better than wrestling with overgrown bushes."

She led Sanford back into the house and showed him where the Santa costume lay across the bed. Then she closed the bedroom door so he could change. She went to the linen closet and removed an old pillowcase. Going back into the kitchen, she began stuffing it with the presents the children had brought for the gift exchange. As she worked, she listened as Wendy continued with his story.

"So Ike was in a real fix. Not only did he not have a stove so he could keep warm, he had let some stranger borrow his sled so he couldn't get into town where he could find shelter for the night."

Mary returned to the bedroom door and gently knocked. "How's it going, Sanford?" she called, her ear to the door.

The bedroom door suddenly opened. Caught off guard, Mary quickly stepped back. Then she gasped. Standing before her was the very incarnation of Santa Claus! Not only did the suit fit Sanford perfectly, he had managed to tidy up his hair and beard. He even had rosy cheeks!

"I take it from your expression that I sort of look the part?" Sanford said.

"I swear you could make a living playing Santa Claus. Now, if you would just wait right here while I get the presents."

Mary retrieved the pillowcase with the gifts inside. After she had handed them to Sanford, she led him down the hall, stopping just short of where he could be seen by the children.

"We'll just listen here for a while," she whispered. "When Wendy is done with the children, you can go in and pass out the presents." Mary noticed how happy Sanford looked. Impulsively, she gave his arm a squeeze. "Thank you," she whispered.

Sanford whispered back, "This is fun!"

Then they both listened to what Wendy was saying.

"Ike thought about the beauty of the star. He thought about the beautiful patterns of ice on the window. He thought about his sled, which had been fixed up and given a new coat of paint. He thought about his brand-new potbelly stove. Ike didn't know why he had been so lucky to receive these gifts, but he was very grateful. Finally, I'll leave it to all of you to decide which of these gifts Ike liked the best."

There was a pause followed by applause.

"So that's what Ike got for Christmas," Wendy said. "Now, buckaroos, I'd like to hear what you all want for Christmas."

Each child took a turn, telling what he or she wanted: a skateboard, a doll, a cell phone. When it was Phillip's turn, he said,

"I want your face to fall off so no one has to listen to your stupid stories!"

"Phillip!" Sissy shouted.

Mary peered around the corner in time to see Sissy marching Phillip into the kitchen. There was the clatter of something having fallen, followed the bang of the kitchen door being flung open.

Mary turned to Sanford. "I think I'd better go see about this. Will you be okay by yourself?"

Sanford whispered back, "I think I can take it from here."

Mary walked down the hall, around the corner and into the kitchen. Before rushing out the door, Phillip had knocked an extra plate of cookies off of the counter. Sissy was on her knees, picking up broken cookies and putting them back on the metal tray.

Mary knelt beside her. "I'll get these if you want to go after Phillip."

Sissy shook her head. "I'm afraid what I might do if I catch that boy. Besides, he usually goes to that overgrown corner of our backyard where he sits and sulks–sometimes for hours."

As Sissy and Mary continued picking up pieces of cookies, the sound of excited children came from the living room. Santa had arrived. Mary went to the broom closet and got a broom and dustpan. While she swept up the remaining crumbs, Sissy took the platter of cookies and dumped them in the trash under the sink.

They had just finished when Wendy came into the kitchen. "A bit of an accident?"

"You might say that," Mary said, going to put the broom away.

"That was a wonderful story you told the children," Sissy said. "I never heard it before. Is that something you made up?"

"That story's been in my family for generations," Wendy said. "My grandmother swore it happened to one of her grandfather's brothers, a somewhat eccentric, old hermit."

Laporsha came into the kitchen, looking very excited. "Mama, look what I got!"

It was a doll, its dark porcelain features so lifelike, it looked like it might sit up and talk.

"I thought I told everyone a three-dollar spending limit on presents," Mary said.

"Well, I sure didn't spend more than three dollars," Sissy said.

"Everyone got what they wanted," Laporsha said.

"What do you mean?" Sissy said.

"The cowboy…" Laporsha pointed to Wendy, "…Mr. Jones, he asked what we wanted for Christmas then Santa came and gave each of us a present, and when we opened them, they were just what we asked for!"

Both women looked at Wendy who appeared as surprised as they. Sissy and Mary hurried into the living room. It looked like Christmas morning: torn wrapping paper was strewn everywhere and the children happily playing with their presents. One small boy was spinning around and around, a bright red sled over his head. Another was attempting to use his new skateboard.

"Justin, not in here!" one of the parents yelled.

There were electronic games, a soccer ball, a beautiful party dress…

Mary looked for Sanford, but did not see him. She went over to Wendy, who was filling a plate with goodies from the dining room table.

"Wendy, have you seen our Santa Claus anywhere?"

Wendy motioned toward the bedroom at the end of the hall. "I saw him go that way. Is there anything I can do?"

"No, I just really need to talk to him when he's done changing. But in the meantime…" Mary opened a drawer in the sideboard and pulled out a small appointment calendar. "…what are you doing on February 17th, my son Roger's birthday?"

Wendell laughed. "Telling one of my famous birthday stories, I reckon."

Sanford had gone into the bedroom, but not to change clothes. He closed the bedroom door, then walked to the opposite side of the room, out the sliding glass door that opened onto the patio, then along the walkway between the McNeil and Robinsons' houses. He found Phillip in the Robinsons' back yard, sitting on an old tree stump, absently breaking fallen twigs of wood into little pieces. Phillip did not hear his visitor approach and only looked up when a shadow passed before him. Turning, he saw Sanford, still in his costume, silhouetted by the late afternoon sun.

"What do you want?" Phillip said.

"I was passing out presents and had one which I believe has your name on it." He handed Phillip a small rectangular package.

Phillip set the present on his lap, then continued to break twigs.

"Don't you want to open it?"

"Maybe later," Phillip said, throwing a piece of wood against the back fence.

"I heard your Christmas wish, Phillip."

Phillip looked at Sanford, about to make an angry reply.

"No, I don't mean your not-so-nice remark about Wendell's face. I mean your other wish, the one you spoke in your mind right before you said what you did."

Phillip flung a large twig hard against the back fence. "'Spoke in my mind!' Old man, you talk as stupid as that dumb cowboy."

Sanford leaned over Phillip. "Please, Phillip, just open your present."

Phillip studied the present, deciding. He tossed it into the air and caught it. "It don't weigh nothing." He shook it. No sound. He placed his fingers in the seam of the wrapping paper, and as he tore the edges apart, there came the smell of lamp oil and spices. Under the wrapping was a small wooden box with strange markings on the lid.

"What's all this?" Phillip said, pointing to the markings.

"They are the words of an ancient language."

"Well, what does it say?"

"It says: 'I am the light of the world. Follow me and walk not in darkness, but have the light of life.'"

Phillip opened the box. The interior was lined with cracked leather and held a small glass vial with a wooden stopper at one end. Phillip picked up the vial and held it between his thumb and index finger.

"There's nothing in this–" The vial began to glow, faint at first but growing brighter and brighter until it was almost too bright to look at.

"What is it?" Phillip said.

"It is a particle of a star, a star that once, for a brief period of time, shone upon the earth."

As bright as the light had become, Phillip could not take his eyes away from it.

Sanford continued, "There is no darkness that can hide from this light. No trouble that cannot be comforted by it."

"What am I supposed to do with it?"

"Pull out the stopper, Phillip. Let the light out!"

Phillip yanks out the stopper and the light bursts forth, surrounding him, blotting out all else. Though he cannot recall standing, he finds himself walking through a thick fog. It is as if he were passing through a silver cloud illuminated by the moon.

Gradually, he becomes aware of distance and in that distance two objects, dark against white, moving toward him. He waits,

watching, excited and a little afraid.

The two objects take on human form. Two people, walking side by side, a man and a woman holding hands, their faces indistinct, yet something familiar in the way they walk.

He knows them!

"Mom! Dad!"

And he is flying into their waiting arms.

His father's familiar voice, deep, strong. "Phillip, my son! My son!"

His mother's tender arms encircling him. "Baby! My baby!"

"You're back! You're back!" Phillip cries. The knowledge brings such joy. "You're back!"

They stand before him, tears flowing, love in their smiles. Yet in their eyes... sadness?

An alarm in Phillip's mind. "What's wrong!"

His father's voice. "Phillip, my son, my love, we can only stay a short while."

"No!" Phillip grips his father's body with all his strength. "I won't let you go! I *won't* let you go!"

His mother's hands upon Phillip's shoulders. Her breath upon his ear. "Phillip, baby, please, please listen to your father."

Despair and rage! "Why are you here if you can't stay? Why? Why?"

"That's what I'm trying to tell you," his father says, pulling Phillip's slender arms away from his body. "Listen to me, son!"

Phillip hides his face in the folds of his father's trousers. "No! No!"

Kneeling, Phillip's father places his hands upon each side of Phillip's face. His thumbs brush back Phillip's tears, then he strokes Phillip's hair. "Hush now. We're here to tell you how much we love you. To show you that we're all right now. To have this time to say goodbye."

Phillip throws his arms around his father's neck "Take me with you! Take me with you! Please! Please!"

Phillip's father gently disentangles himself. "I'm sorry Phillip, we can't. You have your own life to live."

Phillip, looks into his father's face. "Not without you!" He seizes his mother's hand. "Not without you."

Yet he sees in both their faces that which cannot be changed.

"I'll kill myself! I swear, I'll kill myself!"

His father's voice, alarmed. "No!"

His mother kneels, her hands upon Phillip's face, wiping away his tears. "Phillip, look at me. C'mon, baby, look at me now."

Phillip, hurt, confused, finds his mother's eyes.

"You are a beautiful boy. I bet I told you that a hundred times. You are going to be a fine, handsome man. You have a wonderful life ahead of you, and we would not have you miss that for anything."

"But not without you! Not without you!" He buries his face in his mother's shoulder.

His father, standing, says, "Phillip, never believe that, because

we died, because you do not see us, we are not with you in spirit. Do you hear me, Phillip? Look at me, son."

He looks up at his father through rivers of tears.

"Now, kiss your mama and tell her good-bye. It's time for us to go."

"No! Please! Stay a little longer!"

His mother and father encircle their arms around him.

"We love you."

"We love you. We'll always be with you."

"Goodbye, my son"

"Goodbye, baby. We love you so."

The pressure of their touch lessens. Their forms begin to fade.

"Mama? Daddy? Please stay! Please!"

Their forms become distant, faint.

"Mama! Daddy!"

Something pulls at Phillip, urging a decision.

No! He cannot let them go!

Little time.

Then in a small whisper, something he has been needing to say all along.

"Goodbye."

He raises a hand.

"Goodbye Mama, Daddy."

A little louder.

"Mama, Daddy, goodbye."

Louder still.

"Goodbye, Mama! Goodbye Daddy! Good–"

He sees them, for an instant, holding hands, waving back at him.

The light–this time golden, warm, healing–encompasses him, presses upon him, and is gone.

Mary sat at the kitchen counter drinking another cup of coffee. *I'll probably regret drinking this when I'm trying to sleep tonight, but I needed a pick-me-up after all the work and excitement of the party.* It rankled that she had not been able to thank Sanford for his performance as Santa Claus, or to ask about the presents. By the time she had paid Wendell, then said goodbye to the children, he had already gone. All she found was the Santa Claus costume neatly folded on top of the bed.

A car pulled into the driveway, sounding like Steve's. She heard the car door shut, then footsteps shuffling along the walkway to the kitchen door.

Sounds like he's dragging, too.

He came in and saw her sipping coffee. "Is there any more of that?"

She got up to pour him a cup. "So you didn't need a ride home after all?"

"I was right about the water pump. The mechanic wasn't busy, so he went ahead and installed a new one. The car's running fine now."

He set his jacket and briefcase off to one side and sat down on a stool. Then he noticed the dining room table with its remnants of goodies and wandered over and began filling a paper plate. "It must be one of those perverse laws of auto mechanics that the likelihood of a car breaking down is increased by the need for it not to." He brought the plate back to the kitchen counter and sat down. "So did the kids miss not seeing Santa?"

"Well, as it turned out, we had a Santa after all." She explained about seeing Sanford out trimming the hedges and asking him to pitch in as Santa.

"Wait a minute. You're telling me Mr. Woodworth was sick, and this Sanford fellow was helping out?"

"That's what I said."

Steve, looking perplexed, scratched his chin.

"What is it?" Mary said.

"I forgot to tell you that Mr. Woodworth called last night. He said he had to go to the DMV this afternoon and would be here tomorrow."

Now it was Mary who looked perplexed. "There must have been some kind of a mix-up."

Steve took a sip of coffee then picked up a cookie. "I guess."

"At any rate, I'll talk to Mr. Woodworth and get Sanford's phone number. He disappeared before I got a chance to thank him."

"You never saw this Sanford character until today?"

"No, why?"

Steve shrugged. "I just wonder whether it was such a good idea letting a complete stranger into our house."

"Believe me, Steve, if you'd have seen Sanford in his costume, you'd have sworn he was Santa Claus himself."

Sissy walked softly into the back yard, hoping not to startle Phillip. She found him lying on the ground.

"Phillip!" she cried, rushing forward, "are you okay?"

Phillip lay asleep. He had been crying–evidently a lot. His dirty cheeks were tear-stained, his chin still wet.

He must have cried himself to sleep. Sissy thought. She could recall only two previous occasions seeing Phillip cry, both times at the tail end of a hysterical bout of anger. She reached down and gently shook his shoulder. "Phillip?"

He woke, and slowly pushed himself upright. He looked about him, disoriented, still half asleep.

"You were really out," Sissy said. "You okay, hon?"

Phillip looked at her. "I got to say goodbye."

"To whom?" Sissy said.

He didn't respond, but pointed to a wrapped present Sissy was holding. "What's that?"

"I know it's not Christmas yet, but something told me I should give you this early."

Phillip sat on the stump and opened the present. It was a photo album.

"Your social worker gave me a whole box of pictures of you and your parents, so I organized them all into a book for you."

Phillip slowly flipped through the pages. He suddenly stopped when he came to one in particular.

Sissy looked over his shoulder. "That's a nice photo of your parents, even if it's a little blurry."

Phillip did not respond but continued to stare at the photo.

"Well, I'd better start fixing supper," Sissy said. "Marcus will be home any minute."

When Phillip still did not respond, she walked away.

It's them! Phillip thought, his eyes glued upon the photo. *It's them. Just the way they looked before they disappeared into the cloud.* He remembered the words his father spoke: *Phillip, never believe that, because we died, because you do not see us, we are not with you in spirit.*

When it started getting dark, he went into the house and up to his bedroom where he placed the photo album on his bed. Then he went downstairs to the dining room. The dishes and flatware had been placed in two piles on the table. He began to arrange them in their proper settings. Setting the table had always been his responsibility when his parents were alive. As he worked, he softly hummed a tune.

A little later, Sissy met her husband Marcus at the door. She put her finger to her lips, urging silence, then motioned for him to follow to where they could both peek into the dining room. They watched for a little while as Phillip worked, setting the table, then quietly

moved back into the kitchen.

"I don't believe it." Marcus whispered. "What happened?" Before Sissy could reply, he said, "Say, what's that song he's humming?"

Sissy stifled a laugh. "Rudolph the Red-Nosed Reindeer."

The Ghost of Jacob Marley

If you have read *A Christmas Carol* then you know that Marley was dead, for Charles Dickens spelled this out in painstaking, some might say, painful, detail. Marley was dead and Scrooge, through Marley's ghostly intervention, was transformed, and poor Tiny Tim would live to sire similarly deformed progeny. God bless us everyone!

But where in Mr. Dickens' gushing over Tiny Tim and the Christmas goose and young Bob Cratchit's hand-me-down collar does he give a moment's consideration to poor old Marley and the sacrifices he made, not only to Scrooge's redemption, but, as a consequence, to saving many a theater company from insolvency through a spirited (literally) production of *A Christmas Carol?* Who gives a fig that that miserable old Scrooge, with the stroke of a pen, gets off scot-free, while poor Marley is stuck dragging chains and swooning over poor street urchins?

Now, let me acquaint you with a few facts which Mr. Dickens failed to mention. Yes, Scrooge was made a new man, but not to the extent that Mr. Dickens would have readers believe. Scrooge *did* double Bob Cratchit's salary, but he also deducted the cost of candles and coal, with the result that if Bob wished for his family to profit from his pay raise, he had to continue suffering through failing eyesight and chilblains.

Then there was the fabrication of Scrooge's becoming a second father to Tiny Tim. I can't quite blame Scrooge for being a reluctant benefactor, for, truth be told, Tiny Tim was so drippy with sweetness and light, you practically had to scrub the sticky off anything he touched. Fortunately for Tim, all his well-being required was proper nutrition, which Bob Cratchit was now able to provide, with a consequence that Tiny Tim would be able to limp his way into adulthood and a likely career of toadying to his betters.

So, why am I telling you all this? Because I want you to understand that despite having a good P.R. man in Mr. Dickens, Scrooge's redemption was only a partial redemption, or in the words of those consumptive old prunes of the *Collegium Redemptoris*, Scrooge was only "half-done," which meant that I, the Ghost of Jacob Marley, was totally undone.

You see, Scrooge was supposed to be my ticket out of this purgatory of suffering. "Redeem old Scrooge," the prunes had told me, "and we will set you free to do as you like, providing, of course, your ghostly conduct remains within the boundaries of good taste."

You can well understand my joy upon hearing this, and I went at the redemption of Scrooge with all the zeal of a man given a new lease on death. I enlisted the aid of three of my compatriots to act in the roles of Christmases Past, Present, and Future, the price for which they made me pay dearly—as if I weren't already lugging around enough chains to sink a coal barge. Then I got together a group of actors—the self-slaughtered, of which the afterlife is littered—and

assigned them various roles: the Fezziwigs, Belle, Fan, Old Joe, etc. They were, of course, quite willing to work just for seeing their names on the billing. Then I developed my own role, shop testing it before former drama critics for *The Times*. "Mankind is my business!" I howled. (I'm glad Scrooge gave me the chance to work that one in!)

I need not tell of the results of all my handiwork, for Mr. Dickens recounted it with his usual flair for the melodramatic. But despite Scrooges' claiming himself a changed man, it wasn't too long after my visit to his rooms that he began to backslide, just a bit, but enough that the *Collegium Redemptoris* declared the results of my endeavors insufficient to warrant my release, and therefore, I must take on another client. Humbug, indeed!

Seated once again in the presence of that august body composed of three wheezing graybeards, I opened the letter containing the name of my new assignment. Then after various staff members picked me up off the floor and had me re-seated fairly upright, I managed to find my voice. "You want me to redeem…*him*?" (I couldn't bring myself to utter the name upon the page, for it was none other than that of the current President of the United States.) Shouting, I jabbed the paper with a finger. "I've as much chance getting this miscreant to see the light of goodness as I would convincing Ol' Beelzebub to throw open the gates of Hell and set free all the sinners! I suppose next you'll want me to part the Red Sea using a squeegee!"

Well, we dickered for quite a while, but eventually the old warts

came around to my point of view. (I don't care how magnanimous a person thinks he is, some people are definitely beyond the pale. Would that they stayed there.)

"In that case," said the head consumptive, a certain Lord Azrael, who looked more like a world-weary undertaker than the distinguished parliamentarian he once was, "let us give you an assignment which perhaps you *can* handle."

I opened another envelope which he had handed me. "Toby Veck? Never heard of him."

"Mr. Veck has come to our attention because Mr. Dickens appears to be writing an account of him. We believe Dickens intends to title his story *The Chimes*."

A Christmas Carol, The Chimes, I could see Dickens was on a musical jag. "I suppose he will stick us with another Christmas story."

"We believe events are to take place on New Year's Eve."

"And this Toby Veck," I said, warming to my new assignment. "I'll have the opportunity to affect his transformation with a sudden ghostly appearance?" (translation: "I get to scare the bejeezus out of him?")

Lord Azrael shook his head. "Sorry to disappoint, but the case of Toby Veck will require subtlety." Responding to my disappointment, he added, "Do not worry, your powers of imagination, which you so cleverly exhibited in *A Christmas Carol* will surely be put to good use in *The Chimes*."

"So when do I get to meet this Toby Veck?"

"Why not now?" he said, and with a snap of his fingers, I was transported, chains and all, to a deserted London street. It was a typical winter's day in the City: dark, drear, and with a chilly wind I could feel across the Stygian shore. If this wasn't bleak enough, it began to rain, one of those bone-chilling rains that comes mixed with sleet. Would that Dickens would set the scene for one of his stories in a more pleasant clime, say Bermuda.

Before me stood an ancient church, appearing less like a place of worship and more like the castle of some minor feudal lord. Slots in the stonework, reminiscent of those used by archers to rain down arrows on the enemy, appeared to be all that allowed light to enter the sanctuary. The stones with which this forbidding edifice was constructed, were as dark as one would imagine the atmosphere within, this due to an accumulation of soot and grime issuing from nearby factories.

As if all this was not disheartening enough, there was the decrepit bell tower, rimmed with rusty iron railing, and leaving exposed to the elements four large bells, suspended from massive timbers. Atop the belfry was a clock, set in a wall of decaying brick and roofed over with sheets of lead, one of which was loose and flapping angrily, for the tower acted as a wind tunnel, channeling the cold air up from the cavernous sanctuary below. This upward draught was sufficient to cause the bells to sway and the clappers to lightly play upon them. This melodious chiming was the only cheery aspect of this otherwise dispiriting ruin, which no doubt even God avoided

whenever possible.

I had mentioned that the street was deserted, but upon further examination, I discovered a sad human specimen huddled in the narrow doorway of a nearby house, which was every bit the equal to the church in its cheerlessness. I assumed this was my assignment, one Toby Veck. I had the advantage, being invisible to the human eye, of observing him without myself being seen. That he was poor was obvious, given the near rags he wore. That he was dimwitted was given by his not having the sense to seek a more protective shelter. Then it occurred to me that Toby Veck was perhaps a ticket porter, one of those sad creatures who eke out an existence delivering messages. Perhaps he was waiting for someone in the house to present him with a message to deliver.

In an attempt to stay warm, Toby Veck shifted the weight of his squat torso from one bandy leg to the other, all the while rubbing his hands together or sometimes slapping them against his chest. Yet every so often he would wander out of his little shelter to gaze up at the church belfry and to mutter something in response to the ringing of the bells. In fact, he appeared to mutter to himself no matter where he stood, or what he was doing, and curious to know to whom or to what he directed this exchange, I dragged myself, chains and all, to within earshot.

"Bad, bad, bad," he muttered in time to the bells' ringing. "Born bad we are. No right to be here." Then he let out a shriek. "Where is it? Where is it?" Frantically, he spun about, searching the

ground. "Where is it? Where is it?" He rummaged through the pockets of his ragged overcoat, but not finding what he sought, he felt around on his chest then his chin, his cheeks, finally coming to rest one hand upon his nose. "There it is! There it is! My nose! It's so cold, I couldn't feel it, and was afraid it had run away and left me." He lightly caressed this appendage with his fingers. "Ah, good nose! Faithful, old nose!"

I'd seen enough and dragged my bones back to the *Collegium Redemptoris*. Lord Azrael appeared to have been waiting for me.

"Yes?" he said, staring at me over the rim of his wire-rimmed spectacles.

"I thought my assignment was supposed to be human."

"I assure you Toby Veck is very much a kind and compassionate–"

"Mental defective," I interjected. "Either that or a madman. Both, actually."

Lord Azrael leaned back in his chair and rested his skeletal hands upon his lap. "Really, Mr. Marley, I don't recall Ebenezer Scrooge being someone a person could warm to, yet I recall you effected quite a miracle upon your old business partner."

"I don't recall Ebenezer going around looking for missing body parts."

Lord Azrael sighed. "I suggest you best get on with Mr. Veck, who has just been joined by his daughter Margaret, who has brought him his dinner."

Margaret Veck was as unlike her father as a Greek goddess differs from a mangled monkey. Her beauty shone forth despite her being attired in a dress of poor quality, sadly out of fashion. That such a Venus could have been sired by that gnome defied imagination; obviously, the postman had slipped in while Toby Veck was out having a chat with his bells.

These two were soon joined by a young man who, judging by the way Margaret's eyes lit up and the sudden bloom upon her unblemished cheeks, was the young woman's beau. He was not overly handsome, but was blessed with a manly frame apropos of a blacksmith, which, judging from his stained hands and ruddy complexion, he was.

"Oh, Father," Margaret said, clutching the young man's hand, "Richard and I have something we want to tell you."

Toby Veck, intent upon the plate of food his daughter had brought, gave no notice of having heard. I leaned over his shoulder to see what he was consuming with such relish. Tripe! and none too fresh by the smell.

"Father," Margaret continued, despite her father's inattention, "as you know Richard and I have been engaged for several years now, waiting for such a time as an improvement in our financial condition would permit our getting married."

Veck must have been listening more than I thought, for he nodded.

"We've come to realize we're not getting any younger, so why

go on, each struggling along on his own, when we may as well struggle along together?"

This finally got Toby Veck's full attention. He set his plate down upon the step next to where he was sitting. As he wiped his greasy chin on the back of a soiled sleeve, his anxious stare passed back and forth between Margaret and Richard. "Are you saying you want to marry?"

Margaret hung on Richard's arm and gave him the benefit of her adoring gaze. "Yes, and since tomorrow is New Year's Day, we thought, what better day to begin–?"

The door of the house suddenly swung open, and a minor legal clerk emerged who stepped upon the edge of Toby Veck's dinner plate, thereby flinging most of the remnants of Toby Veck's dinner upon the pant leg of his trousers.

"Now look what you've done!" the clerk hollered, as he brought his folded umbrella down upon Toby Veck's head. "You're always lurking about! Why must you lurk about? Why can't you find some other place to do your lurking?"

Shielding his head from the blows, Toby Veck uttered abject apologies.

"What's all this, Filer?" said a second man, standing in the shelter of the doorway.

The clerk pointed with his umbrella. "It's this miscreant, Alderman Cute, sir. He's always lurking about. And see, he's ruined my new trousers!"

Alderman Cute took in the state of his assistant's trousers then leaned down and picked up the plate which still harbored a bit of tripe. Alderman Cute sniffed Toby Veck's ruined dinner then (I kid you not) popped the remaining tidbit of tripe into his mouth.

"Hmm," he mumbled, chewing. "Tripe, is it? Well, let me tell you something about tripe, Mr...." he waved his free hand about, "...whatever-your-name-is. The eating of tripe reeks of indulgence. Have you any idea of the amount of energy required to boil tripe soft enough for human consumption? Why, you could power one of Her Majesty's ships for a week on the amount of coal needed to boil tripe. You could feed an orphanage for a month on the cost of that coal. How does it feel, whoever you are, to be taking food out of the mouths of orphans?"

Toby Veck, horrified by the selfish act he had unknowingly committed, was too overcome to speak.

"I'm afraid it is my fault," Margaret said, coming forward to defend her father.

"And who might you be?" Alderman Cute said, running his eyes over Margaret's comely figure.

"This is Margaret Veck, my fiancée," Richard said, linking his arm with that of his future bride. "It was she who brought a dinner of tripe for her father, thinking it a special treat for him."

"I see," Alderman Cute said. "Tell me, sir, do you have a name?"

"I'm called Richard, sir."

"Well, Richard, I can see you are much attached to this young lady." He chuckled at his own little jest. "May I ask whether is it your intention to actually marry this young woman?" He ran his eyes once more over Margaret.

"We plan to marry tomorrow, sir, New Year's Day."

"Then I shall tell you right now that you must not think of doing any such a thing."

Margaret gasped. Richard was too stunned to respond.

Alderman Cute chuckled once more, then turned to his assistant. "You see, Filer, this is a prime example of the ignorance of the lower classes of which I recently spoke to you."

Filer, who during the previous exchanges had been struggling to open the umbrella he had bent when beating Toby Veck over the head, looked up, confused. "I do not quite understand, sir."

Sighing, Alderman Cute pointed to the would-be-married couple. "You see before you two people who are poor, never to be anything but poor, and who are under the misconception that by marrying they will somehow improve their condition and find a bit of happiness in this world, when the fact of the matter is their marriage would be doomed from the start."

Richard was about to object when Alderman Cute threw up a hand to stop him. "Hear me out!" He then directed his attention to Margaret. "You girl, by any definition, are comely, too comely I might add. But should you marry this young man, in a few years' time you will be a haggard old crone, having completely worn yourself out

trying to put food in the mouths of your six sickly children when the truth is you can barely feed yourself. Do you think Richard will look upon you then as he does now? The sight of your beauty withering away will eat away at him like a canker in his liver, and eventually he will abandon you and your children, and the lot of you will be forced to go begging for your bread in the streets."

Again, Richard was about to complain. Again, Alderman Cute stopped him with a raised hand.

"And you, Richard, I can see by your appearance that you are a blacksmith by trade, the work of which has given you the muscular physique which you possess. Why would you wish to align yourself with this woman who will only drag you down? I am not against marriage per se, but what will she bring to the altar but a full heart and an empty purse? Marriage is a blessed union sanctioned by God, but only among those who have the means to make a go of it. That is what I wish for you to understand. That is what you are both ignorant of, and of which I, myself, have the far greater knowledge. I have witnessed, time and again, what comes of couples from the lower classes who enter into marriage without the proper financial means, and I say to you both, not unkindly I might add, that if you truly love each other, you would be better off drowning yourselves in the river tomorrow than getting married."

A confused Richard looked to Margaret who turned away, unable to meet his gaze. A few minutes ago, they were happy in anticipation of being married. Now, dark clouds hung over them,

darker by far than the actual clouds that were bringing an early end to this dreary day. The young couple walked away, each a little apart, each lost in thought.

"Now, Filer," Alderman Cute said, turning to his clerk, "we are late for our meeting." The dinner plate, which Alderman Cute had been holding all this time, he now returned to Toby Veck. "And you best take this," he said, handing Toby Veck a letter. "See that it gets delivered to Sir Joseph Bowler and be quick about it."

For Toby Veck's trouble, Alderman Cute gave him sixpence, half the going rate. By way of an explanation for this parsimony Alderman Cute said, "Remember the orphans. Were I to give you more, I must by necessity give them less. You would not wish to see orphans robbed of sixpence, would you?"

Toby Veck assured Alderman Cute that he certainly would not and mumbled his thanks.

The clerk had at last managed to get his umbrella open, which he now used to shield Alderman Cute from the rain as they both set off. But they had not gone but a few steps before Alderman Cute turned and addressed Toby Veck. "Have a care with that daughter of yours. She's much too pretty by far. No good will come of her, mark my words!"

Toby Veck lingered a little while, reflecting upon all that Alderman Cute had said. In the meantime, the rain had turned to snow, driven by a wind which whistled around the church and set the bells to ringing.

Toby Veck looked up at the belfry. "Have a care! Have a care!" he exclaimed, in time to the bells' chiming. "Better to drown! Better to drown!" He sighed and slipped the letter into the pocket of his well-worn coat. "Bad, bad, bad. Born bad we are. No right to be here. No right at all!"

"So what do you think?" Lord Azrael said, smiling to reveal a set of yellow dentures.

The truth was, I did not know what to think. "I'm unsure why I have been given this assignment, your Lordship. I don't know what it is the *Collegium Redemptoris* wishes for me to do."

"I would think it obvious. Here we have a young couple, very much in love, willing to make a go of marriage despite their economic state, and now, due to the influence of Alderman Cute, they are considering living out their lives without the blessed comfort of companionship."

"So what am I, a marriage counselor? Besides, I thought my assignment was Toby Veck."

"Ah, but Mr. Veck is the key to the young couple's happiness. Only he has the power to persuade them to go against the advice of Alderman Cute."

I thought of Toby Veck cringing under the stern gaze of Alderman Cute. "Seems pretty much a lost cause, don't you think?"

Lord Azrael drummed his fingers in agitation on the table before him.

"May I be frank with your lordship?"

"When have you ever been otherwise?"

"Granted that Alderman Cute is a pompous old lech, that does not mean his advice is without merit."

"Explain."

How was I to explain to someone who, in life, likely had everything given him on a silver platter? What did Lord Azrael know about sitting twelve hours a day on a hard bench, eyes straining over one ledger after another, ever fearful lest a mistake be made in the accounting of someone else's money? What did he know of the gnawing in one's stomach for the lack of a penny's worth of bread, and this so that that penny might be saved to satisfy a greater hunger, the craving to be free of that ogre Want, whose clothes are in constant need of mending, whose cupboard is bare and whose rent is past due?

"You're being awfully quiet, Mr. Marley," Lord Azrael said.

"I'm sorry, Your Lordship, I was just thinking."

"Would you care to share with us your thoughts?"

"Well, would not it be better for Margaret and Richard not to marry? I've heard it said that two can live as cheaply as one, but my knowledge of marriage, though admittedly limited, is that two often turns into six or eight or ten and each with a mouth to feed. Are not independence and making ends meet preferable to a shared bed and destitution? Perhaps it is better to let prudence have sway over passion."

"I see. And you can read the future? You know for a fact that the marriage of Margaret to Richard must result in destitution?"

"I am only saying that given the circumstances, as they have been made known to me, it would be better for them not to take a chance."

His Lordship sat in thought some time before addressing me. "Mr. Marley, why did you undertake the task of reforming Ebenezer Scrooge?"

"I believe your Lordship knows the reason, to be free of these chains I wear."

"Was that your only reason?"

I didn't see the point of this question, so I let my silence be my answer.

"Very well, Mr. Marley. Then I suggest that if you still wish to rid yourself of your chains, you make the best of the assignment you've been given."

With a snap of his fingers, I was once again transported back to London, though Lord Azrael's voice continued to sound in my ear. "The time is growing late," he said. "Soon it will be midnight and the beginning of a new year."

It was snowing heavily, and outside of a small circle of light cast by a street light, all was black save for the dull glow from a nearby window.

"Approach!" Lord Azrael commanded, and I dragged my chains silently through the snow to peer through the window. I could

make out Margaret Veck, sitting before a meager fire, while her father sat brooding in one corner.

"Margaret Veck is troubled," Lord Azrael said. "She is going over in her mind the words which Alderman Cute spoke. Her love for Richard is as great as the love she bears for her father, and out of that love, she would not have her fiancé brought low through marriage. But, oh! what of her own hopes and dreams?"

"And there sits Toby Veck off in the corner. He too has been thinking about what Alderman Cute said and is now trying to summon the courage to speak the words which will surely break his daughter's heart. If you are to prevent the destruction of the hopes of all concerned, Jacob Marley, you must act quickly. It is past eleven o'clock. I shall give you until the clock strikes midnight and the bells ring in the New Year."

What was it about midnight that was always so portentous? Yet that hour figured strongly in many a story. "But I still don't understand what it is that I can do, my Lord."

"Think, Mr. Marley! Think of Ebenezer Scrooge! Use your creative powers! The happiness of four people depends upon you."

I did a quick count. "Four? I count—"

I was interrupted by the church bells ringing the half hour. I waited out their ringing then shouted for Lord Azrael, but he was gone. Snow had accumulated around my feet. I gave a frustrated kick, and a strong wind blew the eruption down the deserted street. The wind also set the bells to ringing as they had earlier that day.

The bells! The bells were the key! Somehow I must make use of them!

I entered the house unseen. The ringing of the bells could still be heard through the thin walls.

"Toby Veck," I whispered, so only he could hear. He looked up, startled then shook his head and went back to brooding. "Toby Veck!" I repeated, and this time I got his attention.

"Who are you," he said.

Good question. I had to think fast. "I am…the Spirit of the Bells."

His face lit up. "The Spirit—"

"Hush!" I commanded. "Just listen!" As luck would have it, the bells rang louder. "Many has been the time when you've heard me speak to you through the bells."

"Yes!" he said, growing more excited. "But never so clearly as now!"

"Father?" Margaret said, turning away from the small fire.

"Do not speak of me!" I whispered.

Toby Veck gave a conspiratorial nod then turned to his daughter. "I was just thinking out loud, my dear. I'm sorry if I disturbed you."

"I have been thinking too, Father," she brushed a tear away, "and I have come to a decision."

"Tell her she must wait," I whispered urgently. "Tell her that you forgot to deliver an important letter this evening."

Toby Veck relayed this message.

"But Father, it's snowing outside!"

"I'll just be gone a little while," he answered, and before Margaret could protest further he donned his coat and went out.

"Follow me!" I ordered, making my appearance faint. It was a soft glow I had used on Scrooge's door knocker, something like a bad lobster in a dark cellar.

"Spirit of the Bells, where are you taking me?" Toby Veck said.

"To the bell tower, of course. Now, follow and quickly!" A plan was growing in my mind. I would lure Toby Veck to the top of that old ruin, and there in the darkness, with the wind-driven snow setting the bells to murmuring, I would use all my theatrical talents to impress upon Toby Veck the need for his daughter to marry her burly blacksmith. I was actually starting to enjoy myself.

We found the door to the church locked, but what is a locked door against half a ton of chains?

"Follow on!" I commanded, and as we began to mount the stairs to the belfry, the clock struck the third quarter. "Hurry!"

I did not turn to see Toby Veck following up the stairs behind me, but I could practically smell his fear in reaction to the awful clatter my chains made dragging on the stone. "Do not worry!" I shouted, "All will be well!" I rather liked the way my voice reverberated in the stairwell; one would have thought I was Charles Kean playing Hamlet at the Haymarket.

We reached the top, where the wind was blowing half a gale, a

condition serving to further disconcert my charge and to make him more amenable to persuasion. Toby Veck clung to the railing to keep from being blown off the tower. With him holding on for dear life, I amplified my appearance until I was revealed in all my spectral, chain-draped splendor.

"Now listen, you little wart," I roared, "and do as I say!" For added effect, I gave the bells a solid thwack with my chains.

Overcome by my ghostly appearance and the clanging of the bells, Toby Veck fell to his knees and covered his ears. But the fact was I had inadvertently set in motion something I was hard put to contain. Whether it was my striking of the bells, or the exceeding strength of the wind, or the strength of my overweening pride, the result was a sympathetic resonance set up among the bells, causing each to play off the others and to amplify their volume. Moreover, each bell began to swing about like water swirling down a drainpipe, smashing against one another and adding a bone-jarring discordance to the already ear-splitting cacophony. I feared all London would be awakened, that is if the creaking timbers which held the bells did not give way first.

For once, I was thankful for my chains as I ran around the edge of the belfry, using them first to prevent the bells hitting against each other, then looping my chains around each bell to contain its motion. It was exhausting work and wasted precious minutes. After I had finally succeeded in bringing the bells under control, I staggered over to where Toby Veck lay, curled up into a ball and weeping.

"Toby Veck," I said, my mouth as dry as cotton. When he did not respond, I reached down to shake his shoulder. At my touch, he shrieked and jumped up. For an old man, he moved with the speed of a thunder bolt. In a flash, he was at the rails and preparing to throw himself off the tower.

"No!" I shouted.

He hesitated, but just.

"No," I pleaded, "Please, Toby, for the sake of your soul, come away from the rails."

He took his foot down off the rail, turned and looked at me. I was stunned by the words which had flown out of my mouth. Then again, who knew better than I the result of disregarding one's soul? I extended an arm out toward him, willing him to come away from the edge. He released his grip upon the rails, but kept his back against them.

"Who are you, truly?" he said.

For the life of me, if I had one, I could not have told him. Then I realized why this assignment had troubled me all along, why I had floundered, trying to make a go of a situation which, to be honest, I didn't think worth troubling over. I realized how little I, Jacob Marley, had changed from my past life to this. All my clever tricks lavished upon Ebenezer Scrooge had not been for the sake of redeeming a hardboiled skinflint, but only as a means of achieving my own selfish ends. The same could be said of my efforts, meager and misdirected, in behalf of the simpleton Toby Veck. My only

ambition had been to use him and his daughter as the means to finally rid myself of these burdensome chains.

Toby Veck broke in upon my thoughts, repeating, "Who are you, truly?"

I smiled. "Well, surely I am not the Spirit of the Bells." I motioned toward a wall providing shelter from the wind. "Come, stand where you won't be so cold, and I shall endeavor to answer your question." When he was as comfortable as possible, I continued. "As you can see, I am a ghost. While I lived, I was... let's just say I was not a very good person."

"Why must you trouble me?"

I sighed. "I was sent, I believe, to give you some words of encouragement concerning your daughter and her proposed marriage."

Toby Veck placed his hands atop his head. "No! No more words! My head is near to bursting with words, first Alderman Cute's and now yours. Any more, and I fear my head will explode."

I held up one hand. "Please," I entreated, "I do not wish to add to your burden, but only to give you some hope."

Toby Veck dropped his hands. "Hope? What is hope for the likes of us poor folk? What hope has my daughter of happiness when she's not a farthing put by for marriage?"

It was here that, if I had had the time, I might have conjured up some Dickensian scene to show him what tragedy might befall his daughter should she *not* marry, but there was no time to conjure up

such a spectacle, nor compatriots to enlist in enacting it. Whatever hope I had to offer Toby Veck would have to come unadorned and straight from my heart.

"Do you love your daughter?" I said.

He appeared surprised by my question. "With all my heart!"

"And do you wish to see her happy?"

"I would give my life to make her so."

"Then let her marry, for that is her hope."

"But Alderman Cute–"

"Damn Alderman Cute! Damn him and all the self-righteous windbags like him. What would Alderman Cute, who loves only himself, know of the hopes and dreams of those who truly love each other? Let me tell you something about hope, which I assure you I do know something about." I rattled my chains. "Hope is not about wishing; hope is about trying, and from the little I've learned of Margaret and Richard, I judge them the types willing to try."

Toby Veck nodded in agreement.

"Then urge them to marry. Perhaps their union will not be all they hoped for, and should that be the case, then they will just have to try harder. That is how this world continues to go around; it is pushed along by people who try. The tragedy for Margaret and Richard, as well as for the rest of the world, would be for them to listen to the likes of Alderman Cute and surrender their dreams."

There, I had made my little speech, such as it was, and just in the nick of time, for the bells had begun to strike the hour. Only

seconds remained of the old year before the beginning of the new.

By now you are aware that the fourth person Lord Azrael referred to was myself. I believe that, on balance, the purpose of my assignment was as much to put me face-to-face with my own shortcomings, and thereby effect my own transformation, as it was to brighten the pathway for three people from the humble walks of life. I shall have to add "wily" to my list of adjectives when describing the members of the *Collegium Redemptoris*.

Speaking of that eminent body, they have placed me on probation, pending a review of my case. I am confident that the outcome will be favorable as, in the meantime, I have been allowed to go about my ghostly business unencumbered by chains.

As for Toby Veck, Margaret and Richard, if you wish to know the entirety of how things turned out for them, you'll have to read *The Chimes* by Charles Dickens. I will say, however, that following our little encounter on the bell tower, I escorted Toby Veck home where he was met by his anxious daughter who soon had him out of his coat and warming by the fire. There he fell asleep only to later awaken and declare he had had the strangest dream, about bells and a Spirit and Alderman Cute, all of which he put down to indigestion brought on by a bit of beef—tripe to be exact. Then he and Margaret talked well into the wee hours, and during that time he never spoke a word against marriage (though he had quite a few disparaging things to say about Alderman Cute), and again and again, he encouraged Margaret

to follow her heart and to give it up to hope.

This is the truth of the matter, though you won't find it written up that way in *The Chimes*, which Dickens embellished in his usual florid fashion. In fact, Dickens wrote me out of the story altogether, not that I overly mind, for we who dwell in the imaginative world are grateful if only once an author should turn his attention upon one of us, as there are so many wishing to have their stories told and so few writers willing to take up a pen and to put those stories to paper.

The morning of New Year's Day broke bright and clear, and it was a joy for me to travel freely about old London, greeting my fellow spirits as they flew about lamenting the fate of those in need. More than before, I felt a close kinship with them and their cause, which is a concern for the welfare of all mankind, and though it is likely that I still may exhibit one or two quirks involving pride, I believe in the future I shall be a more helpful spirit, or at least I shall try, trying being the essence of hope.

As to that, I've been given another assignment by the *Collegium Redemptoris*, one which I actually volunteered for. The case involves a son feared dead, mistaken identity, and possible infidelity. It will be my most challenging role yet, for I shall have to play the part of a cricket. I wonder what old Dickens would make of that?

The Three Dowries

Long ago in a Dutch village, nothing stirred save a small kitten exploring a hole in the wall of the house of a sleeping fisherman. The hole did not appear big enough for a mouse, let alone a kitten, but this half-frozen runt was desperate, and the warm, food-scented air emanating from the crack ever so enticing.

Finding the hole more constrictive than her recent passage through her mother's birth canal, she nevertheless wiggled and writhed, squeezed and squirmed, until she got one paw through. Jamming her head alongside, she squiggled and scrunched, but the hole would not admit both arm and head. Still, she was reluctant to withdraw on account of the warm air playing over her icy toes. Relaxing, she purred and kneaded the warm air. Then it was head first, nose forward, pink nostrils flaring, white whiskers flat against the wall. Her forehead was too wide, yet she was a contortionist, and tweaked her head to conform to the shape of the hole. Blue eyes bulged, the skin about the eyes stretching like a heavily laden fish net.

After much thrusting and twisting, she succeeded in getting her head through, and it was here she paused to gather strength. If at that moment the resident of the house had been awake, what a queer sight he would have seen! A head, nothing more, projecting from the wall, the absurd trophy of a very-small-game hunter. Yet, to the kitten, this

was no cause for amusement, for now her front legs were pinned and her hind legs so tightly wedged, only the small power of her toes availed her. She gripped and re-gripped the ancient framework until her tiny claws split and the muscles of her feet were racked with fiery spasms. This was a battle between life and death with victory measured by the progress of a hair's thickness! After seeming ages of scratching and squiggling, she managed to get both head and front legs through the hole. Then it was just a matter of a little butt wiggling before she dropped to the floor.

One would have thought that after such a hard-fought battle, a long rest was required, yet such is the resilience of nature's creatures that the kitten was soon on her feet and seeking the source of the room's heat: a coal fire, burned down to glowing embers. The kitten drew as close as she dared then lay Sphinx-like with front legs stretched forward. Delighted by the warm bricks beneath her belly, she began to purr.

How was it that so diminutive a kitten could purr so loudly, loud enough to wake the dead? Yet Kristoph, the sole occupant of the house, did not stir in the chair where he slept. As to this, the empty schnapps bottle explained much, for if Gabriel had chosen that moment to trumpet the second coming, it was doubtful Kristoph could have harkened.

Once the kitten was thoroughly warm, she began to clean her fur, but briefly, for the chalky taste of wall dust recalled her great hunger and, forgoing her bath, she began a search for food. Success

in this regard was doubtful, for Kristoph, a man fonder of drink than food, took his supper at the tavern he had acquired in a game of cards.

But the kitten did not know this, and it wouldn't have stopped her if she had. Sniffing her way across the floor, she came to a shoe, and placing her forepaws on one side, she peered within. In response to her weight, the shoe rocked like a little boat at sea, which it much resembled, for it was a wooden shoe with a pointed bow and a high stern. The kitten stuck her head inside the toe of the shoe and found it to her liking, just roomy enough to lie curled up in. It was a temptation. Still, there was that ache in her belly.

Turning away from the shoe, she immediately began an ascent up Kristoph's leg. She had an anxious moment when Kristoph muttered something in his sleep then crossed one leg over the other. The kitten hung on until the motion ceased then scampered onto Kristoph's soft belly. What a pleasure to walk upon this was! She trotted about in a circle then pounced upon a gleaming button.

It was then that she caught the scent, the same that had issued from the hole in the wall. Sniffing, she moved slowly upward until she came to Kristoph's long, flowing beard. Here was the source of the wonderful smell, a heady blend of many exotic odors. Tobacco smoke seemed pretty much everywhere. The heavy smell of lamp oil was strongest lower down where the beard had been used to wipe oily fingers. Stale ale was definitely heaviest around the chin. But the best spot was right in the center. Here she sat down and inhaled

deeply.

Ah, fish!

Of course, being new to the world, she could not have actually identified this or any of the other smells, but that was of no matter. She closed her eyes and purred, kneading the beard with alternating forepaws until she entered into a state of near bliss, a sort of fish-smell-induced delirium.

But better than the smell had to be the taste! Using her raspy tongue, she licked the hairs of the beard only to find the experience unsatisfactory. For one, the hair of the beard was not nice hair, not like her fur. Secondly, though the scent of fish was generally strong, there was little of its taste. Still, the smell of fish assuaged the pain in her belly a little. It was not true food–more like the dream of food– but it was something. Feeling very tired, she curled up upon the beard, closed her eyes, ran her tongue across her pink nose one time, then fell fast asleep.

Not long afterwards, Kristoph began to stir. Perhaps it was the moonlight, bright through the window, which disturbed his sleep. More likely it was his alcoholic stupor finally wearing off. "Antje!" he muttered, then something about a shoe. Then clearly, "You ol' bastard!" It sounded like a bad dream, but whether good or bad, he no longer slept soundly, and somewhere within his waking consciousness, it registered the small, but unusual weight upon his chest. His eyelashes flickered; his eyes opened slightly, then instantly wide as one word shot through his brain: rat!

"Arrgh!" he bellowed, as he jerked forward. The poor kitten was flung into the air to land hard upon the brick floor. Kristoph fumbled for something to strike with. His hand knocked over the empty bottle then his fingers found the shoe. He slammed it down upon the kitten, but missed. The kitten had not even tried to move out of the way. It was all too much: the cold, the hunger, the hard brick, the bang of the shoe!

"Mew! Mew! Mew!" she cried.

Kristoph, poised to strike again, heard her cries; more than heard them, for they echoed something that had recently been very much on his own mind, and he knew exactly what those cries meant.

Why? Why? Why?

Why is there so much pain?

Why are you so cruel?

Why is the world such a hard place?

Kristoph dropped the shoe. Feeling sick, he leaned back in the chair and brought one hand to the lump on his forehead. Two incidents, which had occurred that day, played over again in his mind, even against his wish to forget them.

The first had been an argument between himself and his younger brother, Matthys. Matthys, like all the men in the village, struggled to put sufficient food upon the table. Consequently, he had never been able to put away something for the future. That is why Matthys had approached Kristoph, seeking money for dowries for his three daughters, who were approaching marrying age. Kristoph

had flatly refused this request, and Matthys, who rarely got angry, had cursed Kristoph and called him mean. Kristoph, in turn, had called Matthys stupid and lazy and had turned away in disgust.

Later, when Kristoph was walking home from his tavern, the door to his brother's house opened, and there had stood Antje, Matthys' wife. It had appeared to have been a coincidence, her opening the door just then, but Kristoph knew otherwise. Antje, carrying a heavy washbowl in her sturdy arms, flung its contents of dirty water at his feet. This forced Kristoph to stop, annoyed that Antje had wet his boots.

"Matthys has gone to market in Dordrecht," Antje said.

"Whatever for?" Kristoph replied.

"To sell the cow," she said, adding, "for the girls' dowries."

Though hardened by years at sea, Kristoph was not a cruel man. Still, the idea of his brother thinking he could get anything for his rickety cow made him laugh.

Antje was not likewise amused. "Kristoph, you ol' bastard!" she screamed. She started to throw the bowl at him, but it was awkward for such use. She took off her shoe and hurled that instead. Her aim was true and hit it him square in the forehead. The surprise as much as the force of it knocked him off his feet, and he fell hard on the ice.

"Go to the devil!" Antje yelled, as Kristoph lay on his back.

In a rage, Kristoph struggled to rise, slipped and fell a second time. On hands his knees, he shook his fist, and called Antje every vile name he could summon from his rich seaman's vocabulary, not

that it did much good as Antje had already slammed the door. He had grabbed the shoe, intending to throw it through her window, then thought better of it. Shaking the shoe, he yelled, "See if you'll ever see this shoe again!" Kristoph stumbled away to his own house and there quelled the fire of his anger in the oblivion of drink.

Why? Why? Why?

Had the kitten cried out once more, or had it been Kristoph's imagination? Either way, he did not know the answers to her questions.

"It is just the way of the world," he said. He looked down to see if the kitten was listening, but she had vanished. Surprised, he stood to light the lamp, but in moving, kicked the shoe and sent it skittering across the floor.

"Meeewwww!" cried the shoe in one long, piteous wail.

Kristoph retrieved the shoe and cradled it in his calloused hands. Two small eyes, reflecting the moonlight, stared back at him. For the first time since his encounters with Matthys and Antje, Kristoph smiled.

"Come out," he coaxed. "I'll not hurt you, I swear."

But the kitten had already suffered enough abuse for one night, and burrowed deep within the toe of the wooden shoe.

Kristoph set the shoe upon the table where he ate, and without bothering to light the lamp, for the moonlight was bright enough, he took from the cupboard a heavy ceramic jar. Lifting the lid, he extracted a piece of pickled herring and rinsed it in a bowl of water.

"Here you are, little one," he said, dangling a piece of fish in front of the kitten's face.

Smelling the fish, the kitten lashed out with a front paw.

Kristoph laughed as the tiny claws bit into his finger. "Not in there, little one. If you want this fish, you'll have to come out."

He did not have to repeat his demand. The kitten leapt out of the shoe and as fast as lightning, tore the fish from Kristoph's fingers. In the time it took Kristoph to peel off another piece of fish, the first was gone.

"Mew!" cried the kitten, looking up at Kristoph.

"What?" Kristoph said, dangling the second piece in front of her. "You want more?"

The kitten made a leap for the fish, but this time Kristoph was faster.

"Mew!"

"All right, all right," Kristoph said, setting the fish upon the table, "I shall not tease a hungry kitten."

As she ate, Kristoph rubbed the kitten's head with a calloused thumb. In response, a low growl issued from the kitten's throat.

"Now, now, there's no need to act like that. There's plenty more where that came from."

Kristoph turned the piece of fish over, for he had already stripped the first side clean, and separated the remaining flesh from the bones. "There," he said, dropping the fish on the table, "that's more meat than you've on your bones."

While the kitten ate, Kristoph carried the bowl to the door and threw the briny water out upon the snow. He thought he saw a light within his brother's house across the road, though perhaps it was a trick of the moonlight reflecting off the window. He wondered whether Matthys had returned from Dordrecht, and, if so, what, if anything, he had to show for his efforts?

Kristoph shut the door against the cold and moved to the fireplace where he stirred the embers and placed a few chunks of coal upon the grate. He returned to the table where the kitten sat washing her face. He picked her up and placed her on the mantelpiece next to the unlit oil lamp. The kitten didn't like being stranded on this high place and voiced her disapproval.

"Don't worry," Kristoph said, lifting the lampshade. "I'll not leave you there for long."

But the kitten would not wait, and leapt from the mantel onto Kristoph's beard then clambered onto his shoulder.

"My, aren't we impatient!" Kristoph remarked.

He struck a match to the lamp then pulled the chair closer to the fire and sat down. "Now let's see how many fleas you have." He found three fleas and flicked them into the fire. The kitten, in response to this grooming, purred contently, then curled up on his lap. Kristoph stroked the kitten's head even after her little motor works ceased to putter and she settled silently into sleep. There was much on his mind, and most of it concerned the kitten's questions.

Why is there so much pain?

Pain and pleasure go hand in hand, he reasoned. That's just the way of it. He thought of the kitten: one moment cold and starving, the next warm and sated.

Why are you so cruel?

He was not cruel, at least not by his reckoning. At least, no crueler than the next man, and he knew men well, particularly those of his village.

Why was the world such a hard place?

Like pain, it was just the way things were. He had never known it otherwise. Yet would his life had been made easier if he had chosen differently, perhaps taken a wife and raised children, as Matthys had done?

"You make your choices and you live with them." Odd this talking aloud, he thought. It had to be the presence of the kitten.

He leaned back in the chair, closed his eyes, but his mind was far too busy for sleep. He thought of his brother's request for money. As a mental exercise, he pondered the amount sufficient for a girl's dowry.

A gulden.

This response coming from some recess in his brain was like another blow to the head. A gulden! A man might work for a whole year and consider himself lucky to have a gulden to show for his efforts. Kristoph doubted he even possessed any.

Slowly, so as not to disturb the kitten, he stood and gently laid her upon his bed opposite the fireplace. Then he went to the window

and drew the curtains, though it was very unlikely anyone would have looked in at that time of night. Beneath his bed there was a brick like all the others, only this one loose. Kneeling, he pried up the brick and removed a large bag from the hole beneath. He loosened the drawstring and poured the contents upon the bed. It made a sizable pile and atop this glittering mound of silver lay three guldens. The sight of them angered him, for it was as if the guldens were taunting him. *Three golden guldens, three daughters' dowries.* He shook his head. How could he be thinking what he was thinking?

He hefted one of the coins. It was heavy, as it should be, for it represented countless nights in frigid weather when lesser men had already quit the sea. It represented distant and dangerous voyages when others were content with meager catches inshore. It represented daring raids upon the territories of rival fishing villages when need, or plain greed, had demanded it. How could he think of giving away what he had come by so hard?

For a long time, he remained kneeling beside the bed, studying the gleaming mound of coins. It wasn't the sacrifice of his hard work that troubled him as much as the fear that one day he might need the coins and not have them. Then again…

"All right, I'll do it!" He stood up and holding the three guldens, walked to the table and placed them in Antje's wooden shoe. "But they had better not ask for another copper! Not ever!"

Before he changed his mind, he took the shoe and went to the door and opened it. The moonlight was bright upon the snow. He

shielded his eyes with one hand as he looked about. Of course, being the dead of night, there was no one about, but under the circumstances, he had to be sure. Satisfied, he crept toward his brother's house. When he reached the door, he again looked around before placing Antje's shoe before the threshold then mounding the snow in front of it so the shoe could only be seen by a person opening the door. Then he stole back to his own house and quietly closed the door. His heart was pounding, his head throbbing. What had he done? He had always thought Matthys the stupider of the two brothers. Now, he was not so sure.

Feeling old and tired, he lifted the kitten so he could lay down. The kitten did not wake, yet it was a long time before Kristoph could join her in sleep.

"Kristoph! Kristoph!" cried Antje, pounding on Kristoph's door.

Kristoph, awakened from a troubled sleep, quietly moaned then rolled onto his side. He wanted her to go away.

Antje rattled the door, but it was bolted against her. She pounded on the door again. "Kristoph, I know you're in there!"

Kristoph was now fully awake. The light in the room was dim. He was glad he had closed the curtains; Antje would not be able to look in.

"Kristoph?" She sounded less certain now. Was he at home or not? There came a lighter rapping. "Kristoph?" More silence, then, "You ol' bastard."

How different her tone from the last time she had called him that! How tender her voice–and something else: Kristoph heard her joy.

It was not a feeling he shared. He lay, watching the kitten at play on the floor. She had found a button and thought this a great toy. She would bat it along the floor, then run after it, take it in her mouth, immediately drop it, then stare at it as if it were a thing alive and might run away, encourage it along with a soft pat, then bat it across the floor and repeat the game anew.

Kristoph considered getting up and building up the fire, but the smoke would announce his presence. Instead, he closed his eyes and fell asleep again.

It was not pounding that woke him later, but his need to urinate. Throwing back his covers, he pulled the chamber pot from beneath the bed, set it on a chair and used it while standing. When finished, he buttoned his trousers, then scratched his scalp with both hands. Now that he was up, he must decide what to do. If he went to the tavern, Antje would discover him and certainly plague him with her gratitude. This troubled him less than knowing the furor that was going to erupt once others learned of what he had done. He realized he must get away from the village! Away without anyone seeing him!

A movement attracted his attention. The kitten had managed to climb onto the table and was sniffing the edges of water left from the night before. He snatched her by the nape of her neck then with his free hand, swept the water onto the floor. Dropping the kitten

hard upon the table, he lifted the lid of the jar with the herring.

"Everyone wants something from me!" he grumbled.

This time he didn't bother to rinse the fish, but tore off a large section of flesh and tossed it onto the table. The kitten appeared not to mind the saltiness, and as she ate, Kristoph cautiously lifted a corner of the window curtain and peered out. Happily, there was a fog so thick he could not see his brother's house just across the road.

He let the curtain fall, then scratched his cheek, thinking. The fog would mask his escape, but where would he go? Then it occurred to him that if Matthys could go to Dordrecht, so could he. He would be getting a late start, but that was all the better, for he was not planning to return until everyone in the village was asleep. He might even stay the night in Dordrecht.

Now that he had a plan, he moved quickly. He pulled on his heavy boots, then took a wool sweater from his sea chest followed by his black wool coat, then a soft cap and a scarf around his neck. He never owned a pair of gloves, for gloves were an encumbrance when at sea, but he had his deep coat pockets to keep his hands warm.

Having completed his dress, he patted his trouser pockets to check that he had ample coin, then put his pipe and tobacco into a coat pocket. Finally, he looked around the room to see if there was anything he had forgotten.

The kitten, having finished her breakfast, was peering over the edge of the table, trying to figure a way down. Kristoph dropped her

into his other coat pocket as if she were no more than a ring of keys.

"Mew!" the kitten cried.

"Hush!" Kristoph warned her. He did not want her cries announcing his departure. He opened the door a few inches and looked out. The fog was now so thick even the road disappeared within a few feet. He stood listening, but the only sound was the intermittent clang of a ship's bell. He closed the door and strode quickly away. The crunch of his boots upon the snow sounded like the discharge of cannons to his ears, but no one challenged him. After a few minutes walking, he relaxed. He reached for his pipe and tobacco, but into the wrong pocket. The kitten pounced upon his fingers. Laughing, he pulled her out.

"Are you ready for a bit of adventure, little one?" he said, holding her before his face.

"Mew," she answered.

He raised the collar of his coat and tucked the kitten between it and the back of his neck. The kitten, pleased with her lofty perch, purred and kneaded Kristoph's scarf.

Kristoph found his pipe, packed it with tobacco, lit it, and drew in the sweet smoke. He exhaled with a sigh of satisfaction. His pipe warmed him; the kitten's purring pleased him; the trampled roadway was easy to follow; and he was pleased to have gotten away so easily. Feeling very content, he let his legs gather in the pleasant miles, and by the time he reached Dordrecht, it was early afternoon and the fog had lifted.

Upon entering the town, Kristoph discovered there was a fair in progress. He did not immediately plunge into the festivities, which were in full swing, but hung back, observing. Vendors were busy selling food from booths. Craftsmen hawked their wares from the backs of wagons. But more than commerce was happening. High above the heads of a spellbound audience, an acrobat balanced upon a rope. Not to be outdone, two jugglers tossed belaying pins between them, while each keeping three more suspended in the air. There was a man who inhaled swords and another who exhaled fire. Music from different groups of musicians reached his ears, wound together in a merry cacophony. How this pageantry mocked the solemn poverty of his own village!

Yet this joyous spectacle did not fuel Kristoph's contentment, for he was a quiet man, an inward man, always awkward in crowds. True, he owned a tavern, but that had come to him by chance, not choosing, and he left the running of it to others while he hid in the storage room and smoked and drank and occasionally played chess with a few old cronies.

Now, as he watched the frolickers, he felt uneasy. He stood in the road not knowing what to do. Having walked so far, it seemed foolish to just turn around and go back home. Besides, if he did, he would return to find his village still awake.

Absorbed in his thoughts, Kristoph had forgotten the kitten until he saw her in the roadway ahead of him marching forward with upturned tail. It seemed *she* felt no reluctance to join the

merrymaking. Smiling, Kristoph hurried forward, scooped the kitten up, and placed her upon his shoulder.

"Very well. We'll go have a bit of supper and some ale. But then we're going home!"

But if Kristoph thought to pass through the crowds unnoticed, he was much mistaken, for he could hardly take a step without someone remarking upon the beautiful, snow-white kitten and asking Kristoph for permission to hold her. For the kitten, this was heaven, for in addition to much petting and adoration, she received many delicacies of food, which forced Kristoph to wonder whether mere fish would ever again have an allure.

As for Kristoph, he was drawn into conversations he never would have struck up on his own, and, to his surprise, he found these idle chats pleasurable. And once he started to enjoy himself, he started to purchase things, and once he started to purchase things, he could not seem to stop. It did not trouble him that he bought the fish pies, or the tankard of ale, for these were welcomed after a long walk and would provide sustenance for the journey home. And a bit of toffee was all right, for he liked to indulge his sweet tooth when he could.

But what of the other things? Did he truly need a new pipe and more tobacco? A new cap? New scarf? Wool socks, perhaps, but two pair? And gloves of all things! And why did he think the kitten needed a fine piece of woven cloth for a new bed?

With feelings bounding between exaltation and horror,

Kristoph passed over his money and received small treasures in return. He was even forced to purchase a basket to carry them all. He knew he had gone around the bend when he bought a bar of lavender-scented soap!

It was a relief when he discovered he had circled through the streets and back to where he started, for now he had seen everything there was to purchase. He found an empty bench away from the crowds and sat down to rest his tired legs and to examine his purchases. Leaning forward he looked with bewilderment into the basket. The kitten, atop his shoulder, looked down also.

"It must have been something they put in the ale," he explained to her. "Makes a man a fool."

What was happening to him? This buying madness on the heels of yesterday's munificence? Yet when he thought about the guldens he had given his nieces, he realized he had given nothing to Matthys and Antje.

Quickly, he rummaged through the contents of the basket. The pipe and tobacco he would give to Matthys, as well as a pair of socks. Also, the gloves. For Antje, there was the bar of soap and the basket itself, which were women's things anyway.

He sat back and idly ran his fingers through the tangle of his beard. He wanted to give Antje something else, something special. He looked to the west, where the setting sun was a watery smear in the overcast sky. With the coming darkness, merchants and craftsmen were starting to close their booths and to pack their

wagons. Kristoph stood, swept up his basket, then strode back into the fair, for he wanted to make one final purchase.

He wandered about in growing frustration until he finally found the wagon he remembered. The merchant, a sad-looking cobbler, was packing away his tools and unsold shoes with the help of his tired wife, while their two small children slept upon a bed of straw in their wagon. The cobbler was happy to unpack crates so that Kristoph could make a purchase. The cobbler's wife helped Kristoph select a pair of shoes to fit Antje–leather shoes, not wooden. Once he paid for the shoes, Kristoph had but two copper pennies left. He hesitated before placing these into the hand of the surprised woman.

"For the children," he explained.

Then he lifted his basket, now heavier by the addition of the shoes, and made toward the road that would take him home. Outside the ebbing crowd, he stopped to button his coat, for with the setting of the sun, the temperature had begun to fall. The poor kitten sat upon his shoulder shivering. Kristoph lifted her off his shoulder and tucked her inside his warm coat pocket. Then he hoisted his basket, and moved briskly down the road, for he had a long way to go, and already he yearned for bed.

It was well after midnight when he saw his little house and the moonlight reflecting off it. He knew it would be a cold house that greeted him, but he was too tired to care. He pushed open the door and, to his surprise, was met with a gush of warm air. The oil lamp,

resting on the table, provided a welcome light. Dropping his basket beside the lamp, he looked around and saw things had been altered. The floor had been scrubbed. The fireplace, which held a good fire, had been cleared of its accumulation of ash. The chamber pot, which he had left on the chair, had been empties and returned to its rightful place under the bed, and the bed made up. As for the bed, gone was the bed cover fashioned from an old sheet of sail cloth, and in its place, a quilt. It was not a new one, yet little worn, and with an applique of pretty red flowers and green vines only just starting to fade.

Kristoph fingered the quilt. "Women's stuff," he muttered, but was pleased, nonetheless. He folded back the covers which released the fresh smell of laundry soap. Carefully, he removed the kitten from his pocket and set her upon the fresh bedding where she stretched out until she was twice her length before curling up to go to sleep.

Kristoph then threw off his coat and, rubbing his hands together, approached the table, for on it sat a pitcher of ale, and under a piece of cloth, a loaf of baked bread still a little warm. Not bothering with a knife, he tore off a chunk of bread and stuffed it into his mouth. This he washed down with ale drunk straight from the pitcher. Wiping his mouth with the end of his beard, he looked about the room and liked what he saw. His mantel, which had not been dusted in memory, was gleaming from an application of furniture oil. The chair fabric had been brushed, and a tear on the seat cushion sewn. Had he been more observant, he would have also noticed a

small hole in his wall had been plugged with oakum.

These many kindnesses made Kristoph happy, happier than when he won his tavern in the card game, and he knew who to thank. He was out his door and nearly to his brother's house before he remembered it was the middle of the night and Antje, along with everyone else, would be asleep. Still, he was tempted to pound upon his brother's door and rouse them all out of bed, for he felt an impishness that was the product of his elation. Resisting this temptation, he turned to go home, but in turning, he happened to glance at the house next to his brother's and saw something lying outside its door. Curious, he went to investigate. What he discovered made his happiness vanish, and his head throb under the pressure of a quickening pulse, for in front of the door were two wooden shoes.

He hurried to the next house where it was just as he feared, more wooden shoes, this time five. Alarmed, he ran down the road and at every house it was the same: wooden shoes in front of each door, only the number varied. Swearing under his breath, he clenched his fists. He should have known that word of his generosity would make him the target of opportunists. Well, he knew just the way to put an end to this mischief! He would gather up all the shoes and burn them, and tomorrow when the villagers were walking about in their stocking feet, he would savor a warm fire fueled at their expense! What a laugh that would be!

Yet before he started to instigate this excellent plan, he suddenly saw matters with a clarity that had nothing to do with the

brightness of the moon. As he slowly walked along the row of houses, he saw not only the crumbling walls, but the people who dwelled within them. Here lived a widow struggling to feed her two children; here was a child with a club foot; here a father addicted to drink; here the parents of two children dead from scarlet fever; next door, a young father on whose eyes cataracts were growing; and across the street another young man whose father had thrown away his son's inheritance in a game of cards. He realized that every house had been visited by some tragedy, save one, the house which he now stood in front of. Why did his house appear shabbier than all the others, for was he not by far the richest man in the village? He opened his door and again was greeted with brightness and warmth, only this time they gave him no cheer. He shut the door and leaned against it. Once again he felt the madness coming upon him and knew he would be helpless to fight it. This time he did not bother with the curtains, but went straight to the hideaway and extracted the bag of money. Next he took down from the mantelpiece a dusty Bible, which served as a repository for important papers, and from this, he removed an envelope. Then he put on his coat, for he could not stop trembling.

As Kristoph made his way back along the row of houses, he placed money into every shoe. Though generous, he did not place an equal amount into each, but where the need was greater, he put more. And into one particular shoe, he placed the cherished deed to his tavern.

When Kristoph at last returned home, he tossed the money

bag, and it hit upon the table with hardly a sound. He did not trouble to remove his coat, but sat upon his bed feeling drained of life. The kitten, awake, tried to climb upon his lap, but he pushed her away. Yet when she approached a second time, he received her and gently scratched her head. Then with a shudder, he leaned forward and to the stain of his beard, he added the salt of his tears. He despised himself for his weakness, yet what was that compared to this feeling in his chest, for a crack had opened in his heart which could not be plugged with oakum, and he cried with the pain of it, and for all he would lose by it. In his mind, he saw his remaining years as a constant surrendering until all he had accumulated by strength was lost by his own weakness and stupidity. Then what would become of him?

Awake! Awake!

Kristoph, who just a little while earlier had fallen asleep sitting up, worked to open his eyes.

Awake! cries the watchman, high in his tower.

"I am awake," Kristoph muttered. Or was he dreaming, for surely he was hearing the voices of angels?

Arise, take up your lantern!

Kristoph stumbled to his door, and upon opening it, was immediately assaulted with a blast of cold air, for the fog had returned.

Glory be sung to you with tongues of men and angels!

Kristoph was right! The voices were those of angels, angels

gathered in a half circle about his house! Still half asleep, he rubbed his eyes. No, they were not angels, though the people of his village looked like angels, for each carried a candle whose light was reflected in the fog, ringing each singer in a halo of gold.

The villagers sang with voices sweet and clear.

> *With harps and beautiful cymbals, we are consorts of the*
> *angels, high around Your Throne.*

Kristoph felt a small presence rubbing against a stockinged foot. He picked up the kitten and placed her upon his shoulder as the villagers continued to sing.

> *No eye has ever seen, no ear has ever heard such joy.*

Kristoph could see the joy in the faces of the singers. Moreover, he felt some of that joy in his own breast wherein, not so long ago, there lodged only pain.

> *Lo! Lo! We sing in sweet rejoicing.*

The chorale came to an end, and there was an awkward silence as the villagers waited in uneasy anticipation of Kristoph's response. As Kristoph surveyed his neighbors, he saw the looks upon smiling faces dissolve into uncertainty. Little children looked like frightened rabbits. Is that how they see me, Kristoph wondered, as a man to be feared? Or maybe they think me mad to have given away my money and feared that, any second, I will demand its return.

Kristoph was not a man of words. What could he say to convince his neighbors that he was not that man he saw in their eyes?

The kitten nudged Kristoph's chin with her head. A little girl

giggled at the sight, only to be hushed by her mother.

Cradling the kitten in his rough hands, Kristoph held her out before him, as if she were an offering. "This little kitten somehow made it into my house." He smiled. "I think she also made it into my heart."

Smiles returned, hearing this.

"I…" Kristoph did not know what else to say, other than, "You all sing like angels!"

The villagers laughed then began to sing once more:

> *Blessed are those who, through compassion, bear the weight of*
> *others' suffering,*
> *Who, with pity for the wretched, pray steadfastly for them.*
> *They who are helpful in word, and, if possible, in deed,*
> *Shall in turn receive His help, and they themselves receive*
> *compassion.*

Kristoph was not a man of faith. He had given little thought to the existence of a God, benevolent or otherwise. Furthermore, he had never asked for help from anyone. Now as he listened to the words being sung, he felt his old self dissipating, as if it were a fog being burned off by the sun.

What did this mean?

Seeking answers in the faces of his neighbors, he felt the divide between them and himself likewise dissipating, and, perhaps for the first time in his life, he felt himself not singular, but a part of a greater whole. A madness had driven him to give away his wealth, and he

expected to suffer thereby. But had it been madness, or was it need, for where was the dividing line between giving and receiving?

As Kristoph stood, listening, a feeling of hope was kindled in his heart; hope not for a future characterized by loss, but one to be greeted with bright anticipation of gifts to be given and gifts to be received, as now, this day, with a sharp joy, the voices of his neighbors, his friends, sang in his heart.

Christmas Tree

I always knew I would marry Jacob; that was as plain as the way to school. Not that I had a feeling of what the English call romance. I just knew that the little boy who refused to play "Little Red Wagon Painted Blue" or "We Will Shoot the Buffalo" unless I was his partner, would, as the years unwound, always be my partner.

In our Amish community, one in five households has the name of Yoder. There were three Jacob Yoders. Nicknames allowed us to distinguish between them. My Jacob was "Ice Cream" Jacob Yoder, not for his fondness for ice cream, but because as a boy curious about the workings of a 5-gallon ice cream maker, Jacob climbed upon a chair, stuck his head near the turning crank and immediately had a hank of his long, blond hair yanked out. This not only caused Jacob considerable pain, but gave the ice cream a throat-tickling texture.

But I had another nickname for Jacob known only to myself: "Ol' Fussbudget," for the way he always fussed about whenever we had to go somewhere. At times the man nearly drove me crazy! A trip to town–less than a mile–could not be undertaken unless he first spent at least ten minutes seeing to my comfort. Winters were the worst. He'd poke blankets around me until I felt like a moth inside a cocoon. And how he labored over the hot water bottle! Wrapping and rewrapping it, over and over, until finally satisfied the heat

coming through the old shawl was neither too great nor too little.

"Jacob!" I wanted to scream, "I'm not an invalid. Hop up, crack the whip, and let's be going!" But of course, I never said a word, for I sensed such fussing gave him pleasure.

I had worse secrets than nicknames, unworthy thoughts I could not root out of my mind. Now, I can smile at such silliness, for God did not make us to be perfect, but to struggle to be worthy. Yet for years, these thoughts troubled me sorely.

My worst secret was not a thought, really, but a place I refused to share with anyone, not even my husband. It lived upon my left shoulder where sometimes I felt a gentle hand resting. Then in my mind I would see a bent Christmas tree, though at other times I would imagine California. To explain this, I must first tell about William Hochstetler.

When I was fifteen–I had just completed my last year of school–William's family came to our community from a progressive Mennonite order in Indiana, one that used farm machinery and had electricity in their houses. Our order is more traditional; some might say strict. We farm our fields and tend our homes much in the same manner as our European ancestors, and in this way, we remain independent from the world outside. Perhaps William's parents had hoped our conventions would somehow bind William more closely to the ways of community. If that was their thinking, they misjudged– not that there was any malice in William; it was his exuberance, his impulsiveness, his endless curiosity that separated him from us, for

we are a peculiar people who shun excess, are plain in dress and speech, and value education only so far as it is practical to our simple lifestyle.

William, by his nature, tested our ways: a colored band on his hat; an irresistible, blue corn flower twisted through the eyelet of his Sunday jacket; a popular tune whistled, walking to church. And there was his love of books, books on any conceivable subject whether approved by the elders or not. I remember the trouble he brought upon himself when it was discovered the Bible he brought to church was a Bible in cover only and a Zane Grey novel within. And I loved him for it, being a great lover of books, myself, and never having had the time to read all that I wished to.

Love.

Strange I should use that word in connection with William. Did I love him?

I look back upon that period of my youth as the only time when my friends, rather than my family, were the core of my world; when I laughed more than any time before or since. I cannot reflect upon that time without seeing William's face rather than Jacob's. That Jacob's father was stepped on by a horse has something to do with this, for the heavy work of the farm fell to Jacob, and, for a while, we saw little of each other. Then again, a part of me longed to follow a path different from the one laid out for me, and that part found kinship with William.

Oh, I supposed I loved William a little: his twinkling blue eyes;

his endless supply of jokes and funny songs; his delight in light mischief. But I was careful never to reveal this love. Or so I thought.

The time came when our youth was nearly used up, time to choose between joining the church or leaving the community for the world outside. A group of us met one afternoon in Katie Beiler's barn to sing songs. I guess we thought ourselves pretty wild, though, in truth, we were seldom rowdy. We were fun-loving youth, making the most of our last days of freedom. The Amish permit a latitude of behavior in their youth that might surprise outsiders. Wild behavior is generally ignored by adults who trust that the youth will wear it out then settle down to the responsibilities of adulthood.

The songs we chose were not those of the Sunday night singing, but worldly songs some of us had heard on the radio while working jobs outside the community. David Fisher accompanied us on a guitar he had purchased–unbeknownst to his parents–though he knew scant little besides how to get it passably in tune. I remember a silly song that was popular then, about a man whose main interest in life seemed to be in keeping his blue shoes clean. To this, and other songs, we made up our own words, mostly about the appearances of certain elder members of the community. David's verse about preacher Stoltzfus' bristly nose hair had us laughing so hard, we did not at first hear the blare of a horn.

When we all rushed outside, there was William sitting behind the steering wheel of an automobile. This was wild excitement indeed, for in our community it is forbidden for members to own

one. William rolled down the window and urged us all to pile in for a ride. A few hung back, but I jumped right in, for I had always wanted to ride in an automobile, my only similar experience being a bus ride to the hospital in Akron when I was six. When we were all piled in so thick we had to sit on each other's laps, William spun the tires, and away we raced down the driveway, screaming each time William hit a bump. He did not bother to stop when he reached the highway, but swung out onto the pavement and swerved around a horse carriage with all of us waving our arms out the windows and yelling like little devils.

While we rode down the highway, singing to William our songs, we passed a house which had in its front window a tree decorated for Christmas. This gave us the idea that we should have our own Christmas tree. That was another wild thing, for the Amish do not make a spectacle of Christmas, and what we planned to do with a Christmas tree I have no idea. Yet we were too caught up in our high-spirited adventure to give this much thought. William stopped the automobile outside Bontrager's woods where we spread out, searching for the perfect tree. A shrill whistle from William brought us together before a small pine. It was lovely: a cone shaped cake of glistening needles and gum drops of hardened sap. But having found the perfect Christmas tree, we realized we had no means of chopping it down. We certainly could not have gone to Brother Bontrager to ask for the use of his ax to cut down a tree in his own woods, woods which, I am sorry to say, we had not gotten permission to enter.

William and David tried to wrest the tree from the ground by pulling on its branches, which got them nothing but sappy hands and fingers pricked by pine needles. Then they pushed against the trunk to uproot it that way, but the tree was firmly held by the soil, and they only succeeded in deforming its straight trunk.

The sight of that lovely tree bent at a sad angle sobered us, and we began to make our way out of the woods far more quietly than when we entered. It was near sunset, and the events of the day pressed upon my spirit. I was coming to recognize that not all experiences of youth are worthy, and that I was ready for something else.

As the others moved on ahead, I stood a moment to watch the long, slanting rays of the sun filtered through the needles of the pines and the leafless branches of the oaks. And as I stood there, a hand came to rest upon my left shoulder. I knew without turning, it was William's. Even now I can recall that touch. It was not a great pressure, but a gentle urging, and I knew what it meant:

Come away with me. This life is not for us. There is so much more.

I was no coward. I closed my eyes and gave myself up to a flood of feelings that seemed like rivers in my veins. But after a while, this surging waned, and I walked from under William's hand and married Jacob, and William went away to California.

From this, then, came my little place, my retreat from the restlessness that would come over me in the years that followed. When overwhelmed by fatigue or the sameness of each passing day,

I would recall that hand upon my shoulder–resist it for a while–but eventually give myself up to its urging. Then, in my mind, I'd see the little Christmas tree, and I too would go away to California.

As I said, such thoughts troubled me, for they felt like a desertion of my family, even a breaking of my covenant with God. Yet I ask you to imagine this: a sweltering day in August when the sky is so dark I must work by kerosene lamplight, and yet the clouds refuse to relinquish their cooling moisture. And I have already canned forty-nine quarts of peaches with fourteen more in the canners, and still there are four lugs of dead ripe fruit waiting to be washed and peeled and quartered into jars. And little Katie refuses to release my skirt, but presses it against the stickiness of my legs. And poor Amos, our dwarf son, is over in the corner where he's been all day, crying with the pain in his bones, and nothing I know to do for him. And standing there with the toddler leaning against me and the sound of crying mixed with the hiss of the steam, I look out to the orchard where the trees still are heavy with fruit, and know that tomorrow and tomorrow and tomorrow, it will all be the same.

See this in your mind, then say if you blame me for imagining myself lying upon the cool sand on a beach in California with a can of cold beer in my hand rather than a paring knife.

It was not until Amos died that I finally released the feelings of guilt that accompanied my little secrets, trusting God would not judge me harshly for my every imperfection. Amos had been my favorite and was twenty-seven when he died, and Jacob and I had been

married thirty-four years.

Then some time later, I again took the bus to Akron, only this time the diagnosis was not so good, though not a surprise, really. As I was walking through the waiting room, after seeing the doctor, I met Anna Hochstetler, William Hochstetler's younger sister, there at the hospital with her grandson who was being treated for the maple syrup urine disease. I had not heard from the Hochstetlers in more than thirty years, for shortly after William left for California, his parents returned to Indiana. As Anna and I talked, I learned that William was dead, had been for more than twenty years. A car accident it was.

I went from the hospital very low in spirit. It was not just the doctor's words. Something was now missing from my life, something I had always associated with William. It wasn't that I ever believed the little place on my shoulder was real, yet it had been something that was mine alone and a place of solace. And now it seemed God wanted me to understand, once and for all, what it had been all along: just foolish dream stuff and never a possibility.

As I stood upon the sidewalk in front of the hospital, I became angry, and—God forgive me—defiant, otherwise, I never would have done it. Across from the hospital was a brick, two-story building and painted across the window of the lower floor, "Tattoo and Body-Piercing." An idea quickly entered my mind, and I strode across the street with a will.

I was met inside by a woman. We sized each other up much

like two creatures from different planets. I had never seen her like, and I'm certain, in that place, she had never seen mine. She was a foot taller than myself and wore the clothes of a man. Her sleeveless shirt was a swirl of brilliant colors, though her pants were soot black. Her hands, arms, neck, in fact, every surface of her skin except an oval which extended from her forehead to her chin, were covered with tattoos of no theme I could discern, but a hodgepodge of dragons, swords, roses, geometric shapes, and numbers. Her lips, nose, eyebrows, and the entire edge of each ear were pierced with small, silver rings. And her hair, what there was of it, for nowhere was it more than an inch in length, was dyed purple and green. She was the strangest woman I had ever seen and, for some reason, I immediately liked her.

I told her what I wanted, and she led me to a back room where I sat upon a stool, unbuttoned the top of my dress, and slid my undergarments off my left shoulder. Before she began, she started some music playing. I expected devils to jump out of her player, but was surprised that the music was very beautiful: slow and soothing like our hymns.

The pain was very little, not as much as the doctor's poking and probing. It was like tiny teeth nibbling on my shoulder, almost pleasant. So, I know it wasn't the pain that started the tears down my cheek. I clamped my jaws to keep from crying out, yet could not control the flow of tears.

The woman stopped working. I pleaded with her to continue,

but she would not. Then I felt her arms around my shoulders, and I was leaning against her chest, aware of the comforting smell of her. I cried for a long time.

Later, after I dried my eyes and fixed my clothing, we walked back into the main room. I tried to pay her, but she refused to take my money. Furthermore, she pressed upon me the disc of music. She so wanted me to have it that I took it, not having the heart to tell her that I did not have the means of playing it. Then I went and found my bus and went home to Jacob.

I bathed my Mary when she could no longer do for herself. And when she died, I alone dressed her body. My daughters were angry about this, said it was their duty and not the husband's, but I stood in the doorway and would not let them pass. As long as I live, I told them, my word is final in this house. They went away confused and a little hurt. I'm sorry for that, but I did not want them to see the mark.

Only recently did I know of it myself. Soon after she returned from the hospital, many marks started to appear on Mary's skin: large dark blotches, a part of the cancer. Yet when I bathed her the first time, I noticed a mark different than the others, up on her left shoulder, a green, squiggly V-shape. Surprised, I wanted to know what it was, yet something told me not to ask, and then shortly thereafter, Mary fell into a coma, and then she died.

But as Mary lay lost to me in her sleeping, I studied that mark. What was it? From one direction, it looked like an ice cream cone.

But a green one? The other way it looked like a tree, but where was the trunk?

Finally, I stopped wondering and gave it up as one of Mary's secrets. She always held a few things from me. There were days when she seemed not to know I existed, but I gladly suffered those days to have Mary as my wife, for I loved her since the first day of school. It is not our way to say such things, but I tried to let her know. I always made sure she was comfortable and warm whenever we drove anywhere. And I knew how she hated to can those peaches, so when the crop was heavy, and I could not sell nor give them away, I would feed lugs of them to the hogs without her knowing. Good peaches they were, too.

Once I thought I'd lost her. It was when my father was laid up and she spending so much time with that William and I too tangled up with the farm to make my claim. But, thank goodness, William went away, and shortly thereafter, Mary and I were married.

For the funeral, I dressed her in her dark blue dress, for I know she loved the color. Then I slipped her white organdy kapp over her head, crying as I did so. It was when I went to the closet to get the apron she wore on our wedding day that I found the letter she left for me tucked within the pocket.

Dear Jacob,
     I want to explain to you about the Christmas tree on my shoulder, for I don't want you fretting over it. You

know I have done many silly things in my life, and this was one of them.

When I left the hospital with the news from the doctor, I was not whole in my thinking. There have been times when I have struggled upon the pathway to God. The tattoo is a sign of that struggle and, of itself, of no importance. I have asked God to forgive my waywardness, and am now at peace.

But it is important for you to know that the tattoo was nothing directed at you. I love you, Jacob. You have always been a good friend to me.

I go now to God's home where you and I shall meet again.

Your Mary

P.S. The next time Annie Troyer asks why our hams always taste so sweet, you tell her your secret.

The '59 Chevy Apache Pipe Organ

It was a comment Willis made that started it all off. We were driving back from one of our handyman jobs—Willis doing the driving, as usual, and me, as usual, immersed in my worrywart thoughts, like how the hell are we ever gonna make any money doing piddly jobs like the one we just finished, fixing some ol' skinflint farmer's bathroom plumbing, which I swear had been installed around the time Columbus said, "How do?" to Pocahontas or whoever?

So, it took me a while to surface.

"What did you say?"

"I said," Willis reiterated, "that's a B-flat."

I had no idea what Willis was talking about till I became aware of a high whistling sound coming from the lumber rack. I pulled my blues harp out of my back pocket and blew B-flat. Sure enough, Willis was right.

"Must be one of those old pipes we yanked out," Willis said.

He pondered this a moment, then made one of his "go-for-it" decisions which, over the years, I've come to fear.

"Make sure your seat belt's fastened, Roy!" he yelled, as he stomped on the gas pedal.

Now Willis drives a '59 Chevy Apache pick-up truck, fairly reliable transportation, but not exactly of the German autobahn class.

"Jeez, Willis!" I cried. "What the hell you doing?"

Over the scream of the engine he shouted, "Trying to find the first harmonic of the overtone series!"

I don't know which got to rattling worst, the Chevy Apache or my teeth, but, interestingly enough, somewhere around 90 miles an hour the pipe started blowing that B-flat again, only this time an octave higher. Satisfied, Roy let up on the gas, and I picked my eyeglasses up off the floorboard, grateful Willis didn't shoot for the second harmonic.

Well, I guess you couldn't call us true handymen if we didn't have a bit of interest in everything. Combine that interest with a lot of free time, a few books on acoustics checked out of the library, and a case or two of Pabst Blue Ribbon, and that'll explain what happened later.

When we got back to the shop we took that old pipe off the rack and gave it a look over. One end was nearly smashed flat and had a small rust hole. As we later learned from the books on acoustics, it was a very crude organ flue pipe. But it got us to thinking if we had a bunch of those pipes cut to different lengths, we might be able to play some kind of tune as we drove down the highway. Of course, we found out it was a lot harder than it sounds, what with fluid jets, edge tones, flues, turbulent flow, and what not.

We took some old black pipe and cut it to different lengths so as to get the different pitches we wanted. These we spot-welded to the lumber rack. Then we rigged stops to the pipes and connected

them using a series of wires, pulleys, and levers to the ceiling of the truck cab–this to allow the person on the passenger side to pull a wire to open the pipe that we wanted to sound.

Now, we could have done something simple, like make a pipe for each note in the scale, but what would have been the point? I mean, underlying this whole project was our desire to pierce the barrier that has historically divided the musician from his means of creative expression, to find that deep level of intimacy wherein the line between musician and musical instrument dissolves into some kind of transcorporeal connection.

Okay, so what we really wanted was to have a helluva good time.

So, we only made up a few pipes and planned to get the rest of the notes we needed by over blowing, though, in practice, we never could get more than three overtones. Of course, this meant we'd have to speed up or slow down the truck, sometimes pretty dramatically, in order to get the different pitches.

On our trial run, the pipes blew the pitches all right, or near enough, but they weren't all that loud. What we needed was a resonating chamber to amplify the volume. We took two sheets of shop plywood and spaced them about six inches apart using some old concrete form boards. Then we mounted the box between the lumber rack and the truck bed and tightened it all down–the theory being that the vibrations from the pipes would travel down the lumber rack to be amplified by the resonating chamber, much like

the body of the violin amplifies the vibrations of the strings via the bridge. However, instead of the traditional "F" holes they cut into the violin body to let the sound out, we cut out the silhouette of a '57 Chevy Bel Air.

Finally, it was done, and jeez, what a sound! The pipes could blow a diatonic scale loud enough that cars would pull over thinking we were some kind of emergency vehicle. We called it the '59 Chevy Apache Pipe Organ, and we were ready for our first concert.

Now, since it was nearly Christmas, we decided we'd make our debut on Christmas morning–Christmas being an especially good time for music. Besides, playing the Apache pipe organ meant we had to drive sort of erratic-like, and we figured Christmas morning there wouldn't be much traffic on the road. Ironically, the tune we chose to play was *Silent Night*, a slow tune with a small range.

Christmas morning found us on that long, straight section of highway 14, about three miles out of town. We had our sheet music duct taped to the dashboard where we could both see it–sheet music being the notes with the pipe numbers written above them and the tempo indications in miles per hour. Willis was on the foot pumps–the gas and brake pedals–while I operated the stops.

The first note of *Silent Night* is D, the second harmonic of pipe number one. When Willis got her up to 30 miles per hour, I opened her up. "Siiiii…." Now that "si" is the start of a two-note phrase that swoops up to E. No problemo, that's the second harmonic of pipe number two still doing 30 m.p.h. "Si-i." Now back to pipe number

one for "lent." Then Willis slammed on the brakes and gave me the signal when he got her down to 15 m.p.h. I opened up pipe number three, a B–"niiiight."

Now, the hard part. Willis floored it and when he hit 60, I opened pipe number two to get it to blow its third harmonic for "all." Call me a fool if we didn't hit that note dead on!

And so down the road we went, Willis ramming the gas pedal to the floor or slamming on the brakes, and me opening the stops. The music was something never heard before–not exactly the music of the spheres mind you, but exhilarating nonetheless.

We knew our problem would be the stoplight at the intersection of highway 71. We were hoping to get there when it was green our direction. Well, it wasn't, but we ran it anyway. Allowances must be made for art!

About that time, I had an inspiration. The part where it goes, "sleep in heavenly peace?" Well, "peace" is one of those two-note words that goes from G up to B. I held open pipe number one and when I had it going good, opened up pipe three. Presto! Harmony! Willis gave me a grin that split his face ear to ear.

Then a third note sounded. Not exactly on pitch, and wavering up and down. It started soft, then kept getting louder and louder. Willis and I looked at each other. Where the hell was that note coming from? Right then, Sheriff Kenner's cruiser pulled up alongside, and he signaled us to pull over. The sheriff got out of his car and slowly made his way over to Willis' window.

"So, what are the *wunderkinds* playing at this morning?" he said.

"*Silent Night,*" Willis answered.

The sheriff's dull gray eyes went from Willis to me, then back to Willis again. It was not the look of Father Christmas. I pulled down the bill of my hunting cap and slumped down in the seat.

With great control, the sheriff said, "Willis, would you mind stepping out of your truck, please?"

Now, we're in for it, I thought. We're gonna be thrown in jail, again. Christmas in the calaboose! Would they let me phone my wife? Jeez! Luella! What was I gonna tell her?

Luella… honey… uh, did you know there's some kind of ordinance against playing Silent Night *in an intersection?*

I looked back at Willis, who was pointing out certain parts of our pipe organ to the sheriff who was scratching his head.

Luella… dearest, guess what? Willis and I ran into Sheriff Kenner, and we thought it'd be nice to give him a Christmas present. You know… clean up the jail for him.

I looked out again, and the sheriff was talking rapidly into his radio. Oh, god! Not good! Not good!

Luella… sweetie, you know what I really want for Christmas is a good bail bondsman.

In a little while, two more sheriff patrol cars pulled up, along with two city police cars and a fire engine. Certain it would be the SWAT team next, I ducked down below the dashboard.

Luella… I won't be coming home for Christmas. No, not next Christmas

neither.

All of a sudden, Willis jumped into the truck, looking as happy as… well, as happy as a boy on Christmas morning.

"Jeez, Willis! What are they gonna do to us?"

"Give us an escort!"

Well, I guess you heard about what happened next. It was in most of the state newspapers and was written up in a national magazine. We entered town playing *Silent Night* with the city and the county's finest stopping traffic in all directions. By the time we went down Main Street a second time, everyone was out on the sidewalk cheering us on. Then, we went up and down 2nd Street, and just for the fun of it went down 3rd playing *Silent Night* backwards.

Jeez, what a day to remember! All the comments we received about our performance were favorable. Okay, a few old humbugs wrote a couple of pitiful letters to the local about how it was "sacrilegious," and a "musical travesty," and that sort of hole-in-the-soul hogwash. But not long afterwards, a few ol' boys started coming around the shop wanting to know how we did it. We even got a few out-of-town inquiries, so I went ahead and wrote up a "how-to" pamphlet.

Now, I think this might start some kind of Christmas tradition, like Christmas lights on semi-trucks, or sing-along *Messiah*s. Just imagine a string of pipe organs mounted on pick-ups parading down Main Street playing Christmas carols. And you could be the first one in your town to get the pipes blowing! For only ten dollars, we'll send

you one of our pamphlets. Let me tell you, it's a real steal, and we'll even pay the postage!

Ike the Hermit:
a children's story

Some called Ike a hermit on account of his living off by himself in a lonely corner of Montana. Not only lonely, but cold, so cold that folks used to joke that Santa Claus, who lived at the North Pole, refused to come on Christmas Eve because it was too cold for him. But Ike didn't mind the cold, and he never felt lonely, for he had plenty of company. There was his herd of cattle. There were Russy and Silky, his draft horses. There were the creatures of the wild: the deer, elk and pronghorn antelope, to name a few. And if Ike ever lacked for conversation, he would simply lie beside the creek and listen to the chatter of the water rushing over the rocks and to the cottonwoods whispering their reply as the wind rustled their leaves. This is not to say that Ike did not like people, for he always enjoyed his trips to town, but he had few reasons for going to town and was content to tend his ranch and let one day flow into the next until he lost track of what day of the week it was and what month of the year.

One winter evening in the year 1887, Ike sat atop his sled as Russy and Silky pulled a load of hay out to where the cattle were foraging. Being winter, most of what was available for the cattle to eat lay buried beneath the snow. As his sled rattled and moaned over every icy bump, Ike realized it would not be long before his old sled would only be fit for firewood.

Because it was an unusually cold day, even by Montana standards, Ike decided to move his small herd to a more sheltered place. This was easy because the cattle followed along after the sled, knowing it held good, sweet hay. On a wooded ridge top, out of the cold air that drained into the valley below, Ike spread most of the hay before turning Russy and Silky homeward. He stopped briefly beside a large willow thicket where he could hear the rustle of wild animals moving about in the dense undergrowth. It was there that he unloaded the rest of the hay, for Ike knew it was not only cattle that had difficulty finding food in winter.

By the time he returned to the barn, the sun had set. He fed and watered Russy and Silky then brushed them until their coats shone. Then he covered each horse with a heavy wool blanket before retiring to his cabin.

But as Ike drew near the one-room structure, he saw smoke billowing out from under the door! He grabbed a bucket, filled it with snow then opened the cabin door, ready to hurl the snow upon the fire!

Only Ike could not see a fire.

As the smoke began to clear, Ike saw what the problem was. His old potbellied stove had broken apart, and lay in pieces upon the brick hearth, along with its contents of ashes and smoldering wood.

Ike stood for a few moments, thinking about his having to spend a cold night without a source of heat. Better that he should go to town, find lodging, then purchase a new stove in the morning.

What irked him the most was the loss of his dinner, for a pot of bacon and beans had been simmering on the stovetop. Yet not being one to cry over spilt beans, he got busy, shoveling out the ashes, smoldering wood and the remains of dinner. By the time he had carried the broken pieces of the stove to the trash pile, the moon was up and shining brightly on the snow-covered ground.

Ike returned to the barn and began to harness Russy and Silky to the sled once again. He had just finished, when he heard a voice calling out, "Hello the house!"

Ike rarely had visitors, especially in winter. He opened the barn door a few inches, and peeked outside. Standing not far off was a tall man wearing a long black coat, which came down to the tops of big black boots. The wide brim of a black hat shadowed most of the stranger's face. The only thing that was not black was the man's white beard, which told Ike the stranger was an old-timer like himself.

"Evening," the man said. "I hope I didn't startle you. I saw your light and figured you'd be to home."

Ike stepped out of the barn. "What can I do for you, stranger?"

"Well, it seems I've gotten myself in a bit of a fix. I bent the runner on my sled and ended up half buried in a drift." Then the stranger laughed, evidently not troubled by his predicament.

Ike approached the man, thinking he looked familiar. "Stranger, do I know you?"

The man smiled. "Could be we've met. I tend to do a bit of traveling around here, especially this time of year."

Ike scratched his beard, trying to place the stranger. A great-horned owl called from atop a nearby pine, "Who-who. Who-who," as if he too was wondering who this stranger was.

The stranger took off one of his black gloves and extended his hand. "The name's Sandy."

Ike shook hands. "Mine's Ike." Warmer than Sandy's hand were his eyes which spoke of good deeds done without expectation of reward. Ike sensed in Sandy a kindred spirit and was moved to ask, "How can I help you, Sandy?"

"I was wondering if you had a sled I might borrow. Ordinarily, I wouldn't trouble someone about a little thing like a bent runner, but I've a load of packages, and a lot of people will be disappointed if I fail to get them delivered."

Ike motioned for Sandy to follow.

"Whoa, partner!" Sandy said, as he entered the barn and saw Russy and Silky hitched to the sled. "It looks like you're fixin' to go somewhere. I can't borrow your sled if there's someplace you need to be."

"I weren't going no place in particular," Ike said, standing between the two horses and placing a hand upon each, "and these two gentlemen will be just as glad to take you somewhere as they would me. The problem is the sled, which has seen a heap of use. I can only hope it gets you where you need to go."

Sandy reached up and shook the sled, which protested like an old man roused from sleep. "I see what you mean, Ike, but as they

say, 'Beggars can't be choosers.'" Sandy climbed up onto the wooden seat. "I promise to have your rig back to you by morning."

"What about your horses?" Ike said. "You can't just leave them out there in the cold."

"Don't worry about my animals. They're used to colder weather than this. Well, as cold, anyway." Sandy reached down to shake Ike's hand once again. "Thanks to you, a lot of good folk aren't going to be disappointed." Then as an afterthought, he asked, "Ike, by chance, do you know what day it is?"

Ike shook his head. "Sorry, I lose track of that sort of thing."

Sandy smiled. "Thought as much." Then he snapped the reins. "Giddy up!"

It was Ike who was now in a 'bit of a fix'. How was he to stay warm with no stove and no way to get to town? Still, he did not regret his decision to lend Sandy his horses and sled. Besides, he was no tenderfoot; he would make out all right. He went back to his cabin, which still smelled of smoke, and gathered all the blankets and carried them to the barn. The barn would be warmer than the house on account of the warmth the animals give out. Though Russy and Silky were gone, there was Soda-Biscuit, his mule and longtime friend, along with two cows with their late-season calves. Ike lugged the blankets up the ladder to the hayloft, then used the pitchfork to level out a spot in the hay. Once he was comfortably settled, he noticed a shaft of moonlight, almost too bright to look at, poking through a knothole. Ike turned onto his side, pulled the blankets tighter and fell

asleep.

It was another light, shining through the knothole, that woke Ike sometime during the night. Ike could not ever remember seeing a star so brilliant. It was a diamond, suspended from the heavens, scattering light and causing spectrums to dance about the walls. Feeling as if he had woken up inside a kaleidoscope, Ike reveled in the shimmering rainbow colors until the angle of light changed and the colors faded then disappeared. Ike was sad to see them go, yet glad that events had led him to sleep in the loft, for otherwise he never would have seen the dancing colors. With that thought in mind, he fell asleep once more and did not wake until the sky in the east began to brighten. It was then that Ike heard the sound of a horse's restless moving about coming from Russy's stall directly below. He struggled out of his burrow, losing most of his blankets as he did. The morning air hit him like a shower of icy water. Oh, it was cold! He gathered the fallen blankets and wrapped them around him before descending the ladder to the barn floor where he found Russy and Silky covered with their blankets and eating out of their feeding troughs.

Ike wondered how he failed to hear the sound of their return. He opened the barn door and stepped outside. In the soft, predawn light he saw his sled in the yard. That is, it looked like his sled, yet… He walked closer and discovered his sled had been painted! The old, sun-bleached wood was now a glossy forest green trimmed in red. And painted on the side was a beautiful bouquet of roses!

Ike reached up and gave the sideboard a shake. The sled didn't so much as squeak. Why, there was even a cushion on the seat! As he ran his hand over the cushion's tanned leather covering, he noticed a white envelope wedged between the cushion and the backrest. He opened it and found a letter inside.

Dear Ike,

Thanks again for the use of your sled.

You know a fellow in my business can't leave his equipment unguarded for two seconds without his assistants clambering all over it to see if they can fix it up. Well, I suppose they did your sled some good, though I don't know about the paint job. Hope you don't mind the color.

Sincerely yours,

S. Claus

P.S. I loaded something into the back of your sled, thinking you might have a use for it.

P.P.S. You should really get yourself a calendar. Merry Christmas!

Ike peered over the top of the sideboard. Lying on the bed of the sled was a brand new potbellied stove!

In no time at all, Ike improvised a ramp then slid the stove off the sled and onto the snow. His blankets fell off as he worked, but

he got warm, dragging that heavy stove across the yard and into his cabin. Once set up on the brick hearth with the stovepipe reconnected, it was but the work of a moment before Ike had a fire going. As he waited for the cabin to warm, he studied the glass in his window, for Jack Frost had been there, decorating the glass with swirls of ice, etched in fanciful patterns. Some looked like long, curling feathers, others like intricately decorated fans. As he stood admiring the delicate etchings, the sun rose, turning the patterns from silver to gold.

Ike closed his eyes and thought about all he had been given. There were, of course, his gifts from Santa, but also gifts from Nature: the brilliant starlight with its rainbow colors and now the patterns of ice etched in gold. Ike was grateful to both his benefactors, and he realized he could, at least in a small way, show his appreciation. He drew down from a shelf his largest mixing bowl and mixed a double batch of pancake batter. As the pancakes were cooking upon the griddle, he made a pot of coffee. Then with a plate piled high with pancakes in one hand, and a cup of hot coffee in the other, he went back outside and climbed aboard his brightly painted sled. On the ground about Ike, gray jays gathered, eager for a breakfast treat. They were joined by blue Steller's jays, a flock of red crossbills, and two iridescent green and blue magpies.

As Ike scattered bits of pancake about, a large raven swooped in and stole from an outraged jay. "There, there," Ike said, "there's plenty for everyone." The very last pancake Ike saved for himself.

But just before he bit into it, he raised his cup of coffee and toasted the far north.

"Merry Christmas, Santa, and come back soon. Even if it's too cold here."

www.ingramcontent.com/pod-product-compliance
Lightning Source LLC
Chambersburg PA
CBHW081153170626
46813CB00009B/3176